A Brief History of
Male Nudes in America

Winner of
The Flanner O'Connor Award
for Short Fiction

A Brief History of

MALE
NUDES

in America

~~~~~~~~~~~~~~~~~~~~~~~~~~~~~

Dianne Nelson Oberhansly

The University of Georgia Press
Athens and London

Paperback edition published in 2011
by the University of Georgia Press
Athens, Georgia 30602
www.ugapress.org
© 1993 by Dianne Nelson
All rights reserved

Designed by Erin Kirk New
Set in 10/14 Berklely Old Style Book
by Tseng Information Systems, Inc.

Printed digitally in the United States of America

The Library of Congress has cataloged the hardcover
edition of this book as follows:
Oberhansly, Dianne Nelson.
A brief history of male nudes in America / Dianne Nelson.
137 p. ; 23 cm.
ISBN 0-8203-1571-0 (alk. paper)
I. Title.
PS3564.E4614 B7   1993
813'.54—dc20   93-809

Paperback ISBN-13: 978-0-8203-3997-9
ISBN-10: 0-8203-3997-0

British Library Cataloging-in-Publication Data available

Some of these stories first appeared in the following publications:
"A Brief History of Male Nudes in America" in the Quarterly,
"Evolution of Words" in the Iowa Review, "Exactly Where I Am"
in Sun Dog, "Ground Rules" in Ploughshares, "A Map of Kansas"
in the New England Review, "Nature's Way" in the Beloit Fiction
Journal, "Paperweight" in Hayden's Ferry Review, and "Simple
Yellow Cloth" in the Fiction Review.

For Curtis

With special thanks to my parents, Marion and Wanda,
to the Utah Arts Council,
and to Ron Carlson

Contents

〜〜〜〜〜〜〜〜〜〜〜〜〜〜〜〜〜〜〜〜

A Brief History of
Male Nudes in America

Ground Rules

_Lewis Houser and his thirteen-
year-old son Nathan were hiding behind a toolshed in the unlucky
state of Missouri. They had been like that for over an hour—waiting—ready to salvage their lives and take what was theirs. "Ground
rule number one," Lewis had told Nathan earlier, "is no talking, not
even a single word because this hot, windless air can take a sound
and stretch it and make it last forever." Nathan was small for his age,
but he understood perfectly what they were doing, and as he stood
there with his father behind the shed he was determined that the sun
could bake him and that he could stand forever and a day on a boy's
shaky legs, but he would not say a word.

From their secret vantage point, Lewis and Nathan watched the
back of the house, specifically the screen door, which had banged
open and shut twice since they began their wait. Both times it was
Alta who came out of the house, first to empty a white sack into a garbage can and then to hang laundry on the clothesline. Lewis noticed

that she was thinner than before, tanned and rather slow, no longer his Snow Queen, no longer the rouged Queen Bee he had married in a six-minute ceremony in Ely, Nevada.

"She's no one that we even know anymore"—that was ground rule number two, and three weeks ago Lewis had bought Nathan a lime snow cone to explain it. "She was your mother once," he told Nathan in a snack shop called Pacific Ice, "but now she's another woman. She made her choices, and they didn't include us. Thirteen is old enough to swallow your teeth and accept that."

And, in fact, Nathan had felt nothing when Alta came out of the house. In the past three years that she had been living another life, Nathan had practiced feeling nothing, had steadily pressed the lead of a pencil into his hand every day of school until his father had seen it, opened the bottle of Merthiolate, and said, "Boys who like to hurt themselves wind up downriver."

When Nathan looked at Alta there in her yard after so much practice, she was just someone reaching up to hang a wet shirt on a line. She was only a tired looking, dark-haired obstacle who separated them from what they had driven eight hundred miles in an oil-guzzling Chrysler to retrieve.

They knew that Todd was inside the house, and they knew that they were in limbo until they had him back—the three of them in the Chrysler heading into a star-topped, million-dollar world where Lewis said their bread would always come buttered hot. The windows in the house were open, and soon after they arrived at their point of surveillance Lewis and Nathan had heard the TV from inside, something that sounded like cartoons—a duck talking, a woodpecker going crazy on a tree. Lewis had turned to Nathan and pointed at his own ear, and Nathan shook his head yes in response, signaling that he'd heard it, too.

Standing silent as grass, their cotton shirts sweated through, they waited in their place and became familiar with ground rule number three—invisibility. At first Nathan could not imagine being a ghost, but that's how his father had described it. "No one can see us. Everything has to be done in the blink of a blue eye." They had bulldozed the brown getaway Chrysler into a hearty stand of sumac just down the road so that the car became invisible as well, vinyl top and rust spots lost to the dense Midwestern cover. Now they stood at the very edge of the toolshed in a hairline margin of safety where they could watch the house but still remain unseen. "One careless move, a sneeze or even a cough could ruin everything," Lewis had warned Nathan, but Nathan had sworn he could do it, he could be a ghost, he could swallow a sneeze, he could bite a crouping cough back for hours.

"Know what a felony is?" Lewis had asked Nathan while changing the plugs on the Chrysler weeks ago. Nathan thought his father had said melody, so he answered yes. Lewis nodded and bent back over the engine, which was a place of comfort for him—gaskets and pinpoint metal and the high frequency belts humming when all was right.

There was no such comfort in Alta's yard, behind the toolshed, where the two of them shifted their weight from leg to leg. Lewis had shown Nathan how to stand loose, how to relax and let his arms hang like riffraff, but at the least sound or signal they were to cock their heels and get eagle-eyed, quick. "Don't keep time or it'll wind up keeping you," Lewis had warned Nathan. An hour—which they had not tracked—in the midday sun had turned even their hair hot, and when Nathan moved his hand to the top of his head to shield it for a moment, Lewis shook his head back at Nathan in a hard no.

Shortly after that the back door opened with a dull scraping for the third time, and Todd walked down the limestone steps. Neither Lewis nor Nathan had seen him in three years, but both of them knew the towheaded four-year-old in an instant. They had lived their lives for him, driven across three states, and spent hours rehearsing a plan that was skintight and urgent. They had let go of everything back then— Alta and the house in Durango and the easy constellation that the four of them had once made—except Todd, the baby, whom they could not forget. He had been too tiny then, just honeycomb wrapped in a blanket, but now he was halfway to Lewis's waist and had more than a fighting chance.

Todd lingered on the steps, looking down at his bare feet, and for both Lewis and Nathan that was the most difficult moment, the future flickering but not quite there. Nathan held his breath and looked at his father—the lead man, the ball in the socket of this operation—who crouched now, concentrating, calculating the distance and multiplying it by their adrenalin.

Then slowly, like someone in a wavy dream, Todd took three steps toward the yard. There was a tricycle in the grass and the bright, plastic pieces of some former toy. Lewis lifted his hand, made a fist, and he and Nathan went running, skimming the ground really, moving in what Lewis had described to Nathan as a "moment's opportunity—sometimes a crack no wider than a jarred window through which the rest of your life might be waiting."

Nathan was at Lewis's side, not a follower now, but a thinking, running, feeling shadow who saw the expanse of grass between him and his brother Todd as a long, green tunnel, the sky above as a blue corral. And it was then, suddenly, that Nathan thought of himself as a horse—long-legged and filled with lightning. "Don't think about your feet, or you'll monkey-wrench yourself," his father had told him, and now, moving closer and closer to their target, Nathan doubted that he even had feet, except for the presence of his shoes. They were girls' high-top Keds, and it was the only thing in all the world that he resented his father for.

If Alta had looked out the kitchen window then, she might have seen something shimmering, something in a mad hundred-yard dash, white heat waves, or just a man and a boy, but Alta was making beds, struggling with a sheet to make a tight hospital fit.

Outside, Lewis picked the boy up, the towhead, the astonished baby whose face, Lewis could see now, was still sweet and small as an egg. Todd weighed forty pounds, Lewis guessed, as much as a wet shepherd pup, and Lewis pulled him tight to his chest, in love, yes, but also in strategy—no kicking, no chance to get away. He covered Todd's mouth with his hand, not a thing he liked to do, but the windows were open and Alta had three ears and eyes in the back of her head and one time claimed ESP during her period. Lewis had doubted that, but he also knew that Alta was capable of surprises, like the day she had just up and packed two suitcases, some guy with slicked back hair waiting for her out front in a Wagoneer. Lewis had calmly walked out there and told him to get off the property; he could wait for Alta out on the road at the gate.

In all of it—the plan to get their lives back—Lewis and Nathan never stopped running: across the yard, then down for the boy, up and over the back hillside, and finally toward the car. "Fly," Lewis had told Nathan, and he said it just the way Nathan thought the word should be said: spellbound, drawing the sound out into thin air. "Leave a footprint," Lewis had warned in the early stages, "and that's as good as a letter of introduction. Make a leaf fall, and our butts are instantly stewed."

So they were ghosts and birds, not the two of them, but three now, plowing through the Missouri countryside, which was not a landscape made for speed, covered, as it was, with thistles and cottonwood seedlings and brush. Lewis and Nathan were breathing hard, looking ahead for the car, though Lewis knew, every minute, every second, just where they were. For an instant he looked down at Todd in his arms, and the thing about being a father which he had felt before at unexpected times—like electricity, like biting on a hot bare wire— ran through him.

Minutes later, days later—Nathan thought of it as years—they arrived at the car, which Lewis had said only a wisenheimer would see as safety. They hurriedly got in and anchored Todd between them on the front seat, and with his mouth finally uncovered he started his eight hundred miles of whimpering, "Mama, mama, mama"—a cry in triplicate that would seep, eventually, into Nathan's every dream.

"Ground rule," Lewis told both boys after an unfriendly Dairy Queen waitress had handed them melting Buster Bars in the bare little town of Sedalia. "Don't look back. Do what's necessary, then barrel like an ox toward Christmas."

"Chryslers, unfortunately, beg to be seen," Lewis told his sons, and so they drove the back roads, viewing the most plug-ugly state Lewis and Nathan had ever witnessed—big, muddy rivers and a played-out sky. Late afternoon came and then twilight, and finally Lewis looked over and saw that both boys were asleep, rag soft and contorted on the seat next to him, boys who could fill up a space, make it fit their own needs. As he drove, he kept looking over at them, at the blonde baby and the dark, well-lessoned thirteen-year-old, and he imagined everything they would do: ski and rebuild engines, hang a Christmas piñata from the back tree, they would swim and cook eggs with Tabasco, grow some Indian corn. On and on it went in Lewis's mind until he grew tender with the largeness of their lives, until sometime after midnight—the boys still sleeping, the chain link of stars glimmering above—they crossed the line into the sweet, big grainbelt of Kansas.

A Brief History of
Male Nudes in America

They step from behind my
mother's shower curtain, pose like acrobats and soldiers, they lie
bound in the afternoon light of our downstairs bedroom. There are
buttons on the floor. Someone's wallet on the dresser. On the back of
a chair, a shirt leaves everything to the imagination. The shirt is blue,
it is Oxford, it has sweat rings, a pocket, it's a workshirt with the
smell of hay still in it, it's khaki, short sleeved, long sleeved, on the
back *Sugarloaf Bowl* is machine embroidered with *Del Rio* below it.

I have my eyes open. I see them strut. I see them scurry from
the bathroom back to my mother's bed, their big white butts trail-
ing our household like bad winter colds. My mother is divorced and
entertains at odd hours.

I get home from school and on the kitchen counter she has a peanut butter sandwich for me or Hostess Snowballs, raisins, applesauce,
or a Mars Bar. Under her closed bedroom door there is a crack of
light that reminds me of the depths to which we all fall, given time,

given enough rope and the disposition for making our own sorrow and then lying in it.

Karl Winckelman's truck is parked out front. My mother's Sheffield bedspread is probably folded back, in thirds, to the end of her bed where it is a silky white margin she tells Karl to keep his feet off. He has undoubtedly come here straight from work. As a construction foreman, Karl sometimes has the option of leaving his job early, and on those occasions he is in my mother's arms by two, the bedspread folded cleanly back by three when I get off the Highland Park High School bus. Karl and my mother move with the scheduled certainty of trains. No sound. The light from beneath my mother's door makes a line of chalk that divides our world—on this side the radio drones and on that side all reason is immediately abandoned. By four they're standing in the kitchen asking me about homework.

"Hey, kiddo," Karl says, pointing at my opened math book. "I have a way of multiplying with my fingers."

For a simple man, Karl confuses me frequently and with great enthusiasm. He goes to work with his fingers, showing seven times six, eight times nine, how you get wild dogs to cross the street, how you get a scaffold to dance down the side of a building.

Karl leans against the refrigerator, and I can see exactly what my mother has had that afternoon: shadow and dark eyes, a square jaw, Noah sleeping with his legs wide apart. In the downstairs bedroom in the afternoon light, Karl stretches out beside my mother and turns white, blank as snow gathering snow, big as a barn, his heart racing on a fool's errand all for my mother.

"I'll tell you one thing," he says, his tanned forehead wrinkling as a prelude to some deep thought. "The day they turn our numbers metric is the day I stop paying union dues. Can you imagine a 2- × 3-meter window? Come on!"

Karl is like a feed bag with a little hole in the corner spilling its contents slowly. Twopenny nails drop from his pockets onto our wood floors or behind the couch cushions. When he walks, his Red Wing boots leave footprints of fine dust picked up from various construction sites.

"Ahhh, look Karl," my mother says, thumbing his tracks caught in sunlight on the newly polished floor.

"What, babe, what?" Karl asks, and there is a real possibility that this man sees nothing, that dust is a given, maybe even the essential ingredient of his world.

"Karl's a darn hard worker," my mother says to me, which is a way of explaining his presence in her bed, though we never talk directly of her bed—a place of sleep and haste and desolation. The expensive Sheffield bedspread cannot change that. Neither can the book she always keeps at her bedside, *Egypt in Its Glory,* an oversized photojournal she ordered from C. C. Bostwick's. My mother gets lost in that book—the beauty of the pyramids, the secrets of papyrus scrolls.

I imagine on their better afternoons that Karl takes my mother somewhere down the Nile, that the waters are soft, that the meloncolored sand eases them from their real lives. Birds stand on one leg. Marble cows low into the ancient moonlight.

Even with his pants down, Karl is all business. My mother has told me this as she sits with a cup of coffee, maybe picking at a cinnamon bun. I know that in the same way Karl creates a building out of rolled-up blueprints he engineers some deep and mysterious pleasure in my mother. I see her walk out of her bedroom with him, and she is flushed, something has been shaken loose, and for a half hour or more she is truly happy. She sits on the kitchen cabinet and eats Fruit Loops out of the box.

My mother doesn't mind discussing her life with me—an only child, a girl already taller than her mother. She explains sex as biology by candlelight. She describes her need and desire as electric impulses that are strong enough to roll a rock uphill. She characterizes her love of men as something that happened to her in the cradle when her mother's back went bad and it was her daddy who held her against his rock chest and in his warm water hands.

She laughs and tells me that Karl likes her on top where he says she is pretty as a cream puff, though I tend to imagine her at that moment as wild-eyed and breathless—something stunned by headlights in a dark night. I don't know why my mother finds no lasting peace.

"Hey, nothing in this life is perfect," she says more times than I can remember. It's meant as the kind of fleshy advice gained through experience, but, in fact, it's a statement my mother repeats so she will believe it. My mother's voice is strong, deep and assuring, but because I am her daughter—conceived on Chinese New Year, she tells me—I can hear the uncertainty. Sometimes when she's talking, if I close my eyes and drift, all I hear is bathwater running.

～～～～～～

Karl is not the only one. I see the legs of men and bulls traipsing around our kitchen, looking for something to eat. They work up appetites at our house—man-sized. Cans of tuna, a dozen eggs, a raw red onion sliced thick—I've seen them make sandwiches I couldn't get my hands around.

My mother stands off to the side, sweet in a brocade robe or sexy in a yellow lotto T-shirt, and watches them work her kitchen with the sudden dexterity of hungry men. She points to where the crackers are. She shrugs when she's informed that we are out of milk.

In her way, my mother likes them all. It's not for money that she takes them to her bed, but for lack of words, for something gone wrong with my father that she has no way of explaining. He sometimes calls me from Newark to say hi. He asks me if I'm doing O.K.

"Sure," I say. "Great."

Karl asks me if I've finished my homework. Barry Rivers asks me where I got my green eyes; Tim French, if there are any more clean towels; a one-night Cuban musician, if our dog bites.

I want to tell the musician, "Yeah, he'll take your damn head off," but I answer, "No, never has before."

It's my mother who asks me to help her with Manny Del Rio. Sometime after eleven or twelve she comes into my bedroom and shakes me hard out of sleep. "April," she says, "April, come help me with Manny. I think he's hurt."

It's a Thursday night. This I am sure of because Manny bowls mixed league on Thursdays at Sugarloaf Bowl, then comes by our house for my mother's three-bean soup. Friday mornings he's usually still here. My mother tiptoes out of her room and signals me with one finger to her lips, a sign that has come to mean that all the men of the world are asleep, that they are dear to us in that state, camped out and heavy on our sheets.

In the bottom of our shower that Thursday night, Manny is all flesh—the torso of a grand duke and the short stocky legs of a pipe fitter. He looks up at us out of too much pain to be embarrassed.

"Where does it hurt?" my mother asks him.

Manny cannot decide. He groans, then curses in Spanish. The bar of soap is still under his right foot, the water still beaded across his chest and on his neck.

There is a way to stare politely, and I know how to do it, I've practiced, and I think it's fair to say I'm an expert with my eyes. I give Manny a slow once-over, and I see it all: the broad chest, the narrow hips, wet hair, the story of his life pink and small and lying to the side. I look up at my mother, who hovers over Manny like a dark angel, and maybe it's because I'm still sleepy, but it seems as if we are moving underwater—our hands slow, almost helpless.

"Is it your leg?" I ask Manny, trying to clarify the middle of this crazy night. "Your back? Your arm?"

There is an unbelieving look on his face as my mother and I attempt to pull him out of the shower and onto the cold linoleum floor. "Don't," he tells us. It's as much as he can get out of his mouth at once. Spread, exhausted, Manny lies still and poses for us in our own bathroom, his hip shattered, though none of us will know this until later, after he is picked up by an ambulance and X-rayed at Stormont Vail.

We cover him with a blanket and wait for the paramedics. It seems like a long wait, the three of us in one small room, Manny's hand squeezing the side of the tub in a sad gesture that I can't forget. He is a sweet old-fashioned guy who blushes at a kiss but loves my mother with the force of a bazooka.

We wait forever, which indicates how time passes in this house. My mother flicks her cigarette ashes into the bathroom sink. Realizing that silence is the best alternative here, she stops talking. Her cigarette, then hand, then arm move in one gentle line from knee to mouth and mouth to knee. She exhales with the deepest sigh, one that says life simply cannot be lived this way anymore.

———————

Fat boy cupids, men of stone, athletes, bathers—they kiss and fondle my mother, then give me a sidelong glance. "This is April," she tells them in the way of an introduction. "She's on the honor roll, she's in the choir. You can't slip anything by her, so don't even try. Look at that smile. She's gonna break some hearts in her time, huh?"

Late night or midmorning Judy Garland sings "You made me love you" off one of our old scratchy albums. They are mesmerized. Karl leans his head back in the brown easy chair, closes his eyes, and commits himself to that long languorous kind of beauty. "It's only a song," I tell him. Tim French, in his boxer shorts, does a simple little four-step right there in the living room. He doesn't need a partner. He moves unselfconsciously, and everything moves with him—mind and body, dream and daylight.

At the top of the stairs or in the kitchen doorway, I am where I can see it all: Tim dancing in his own arms, Manny searching for his socks bare-assed, Barry scratching himself as he reads the newspaper. It is a precarious view for a seventeen-year-old. My mother pulls me close to her and says, "You just as well know now." We stand and watch in the doorway together, at the top of the stairs, near the piano, next to her bed, by a chair, by a blanket, by a rug, and in the deepest sense they are beyond us, these men who come visiting.

They step out of their clothes or my mother undresses them, and in the golden light of the Nile they are the bare figures of love and promise. In my mother's care, they see themselves twice their real size, agile, long-limbed, generous, hung like bulls, sweet as new fathers. They are fast to sleep and slow to awaken. She tiptoes out of her room in the mornings and puts her finger to her lips and our world is more quiet than the dark high rafters of a tomb.

I never ask her why, and lately I never ask her who. Karl, Blair, Manny . . . men come and go according to a calendar that only my mother's heart could know.

⁓⁓⁓⁓

Laureano, the Cuban musician, drums our coffee table until we have memorized the Latin beat, which he says is the same beat as the heart pumping—da dum, da dum. "That's why you can't ignore Latin music," he tells my mother and me, "because it's the same music as your own body." He taps the left side of his chest where supposedly he has a heart, then winks and stretches out on the couch, dark and suggestive as deep woods. He has grown to love America, he says.

Laureano is a one-nighter, a first and last course all rolled into one. My mother glows for him. She walks across the floor gently, as if it could fall in at any minute. She has filed her fingernails and painted them a soft pastel. She crosses her legs and taps her foot, anxiously pushing the night forward to the moment when she pulls back the bedspread and the air goes thin. My mother will not be satisfied until she has pulled every star from the sky.

Upstairs, in my own bed, I give ten-to-one odds that Laureano will not even show for breakfast.

Mornings are the worst. Everything from the night before has been used up, and it's like starting over. Our lives begin with bare sunlight creeping over the floor, inch by inch. We drink strong black coffee and keep an edgy silence. We are trying not to wake someone, but I can't remember who. Manny? Blair? Tim? They are mostly versions of the same body that scoot from my mother's bed into the bathroom for an early morning pee.

Laureano strolls, and when he looks up and sees me at the end of the hallway he stops short of the bathroom, leans against the wall, and smiles at me with the quick self-assuredness of a lion tamer. I have eyes and I use them. His body is tall and lean—a pen and ink sketch. He moves his left arm slowly up the wall as if he's reaching for something, but nothing is there. He is casual in his nakedness, confident in this small makeshift love scene. I figure it's my hallway, though, so I stare him down. My trick is to stare at the wall just behind him— try to blister the cool white paint. Laureano finally laughs, snaps the spell, and moves with no hurry to the bathroom.

Evenings I sit at a desk in a corner of the living room that my mother insists on calling the study. I open my books and lose myself in homework, in thick black strings of numbers and in the pages of history where fate is swift and lives are not left to sputter and tumble. The yellow pencil in my hand guides me through the night, through the opening and closing of my mother's bedroom door, and through the dull watery sounds of people in the next room.

It's late when she stands over me and says I'm going to ruin my eyes, but she's wrong. I can see every nail hole and scrape on these walls, I can see the smallest cigarette burn in the sofa, dust in the corner, a finger-length cobweb in the windowsill. I can see the storm that has crossed my mother's face and left it soft and sleepy—obscured as if by the distance of an ocean.

There is a place in me—just under my skin—where everything and everyone from this house is distinctly remembered.

There are the long muscular arms of David, who sprays our house for termites in early spring. Under the eaves and around the base-boards, David has the golden reach of a boxer. He swears we won't smell a thing. My mother stretches the truth, tells David that she's seen the signs of termites: a bleached sawdust leaking where the walls meet. He's standing on a ladder, and she looks up at him, her hair shining like a new quarter.

I can see Gregory's back and my mother, kissing his vertebrae one by one, careful and removed as a lady-in-waiting. She won't let him turn around. He must endure what he is made of.

I remember the strong Norman legs of my grandfather who visits us from Idaho and lounges all day in his robe, pockets full of Oreos, a milk ring on the table.

I see shoulders without their wings. I remember a bruise as a place to be kissed. I recall Tony Papineau building a birdhouse in our back-yard so our winter would be crossed with sparrows. My mother wears a green wool jacket and as his hammer sings she dances for Tony in the cold.

I love the way that pages in a book feel: smooth and cold, the edges sharp enough to draw blood. My mother licks her fingers before she turns the pages of a book. "Easier that way," she says. She reads about the far-away and long-ago, about primitives terrorized by the moon.

When I open a book I want facts, dates, the pure honesty of num-bers. I want a paragraph faithful enough to draw me away from what's going on in the next room: my mother dragging herself to the bottom, some man thinking it is love.

Blair makes the sound of a wounded duck, which is the combination of a honk and a wheeze. It is not something I would equate with passion, not a sound that I think of in response to my mother's pear-colored skin. In the room next to theirs, I am reading, studying, fighting my way into a book, and that sound goes on forever. The walls of this house aren't thick enough to keep that kind of sadness contained.

I'm sitting at the desk with the English book in my hands, though it just as well be a jellyfish or a brick. The noise goes higher, louder, the duck becomes inconsolable. I strain, but the words on the page are futile hash marks.

Ten steps and I am at the front door, then out into the night, walking as quickly as I can. I live on an old quiet street that's blessed with big trees and where people still use push mowers. The houses are nothing special—bland with red brick, too symmetric with their sidekicker porches. I know some of the names here: Peterson, Barnett, Stanopolous. The only time I've seen the police on this street is the afternoon that Nelda Peterson's eighty-year-old mother fell flat dead in the azaleas and lay there like she was floating until her son-in-law came home that night. That's the only fatality I know of on this street—that is, if you don't count my mother.

When I get to the end of our block, I turn around, and back there is our house—2431—and from this distance my mother's lighted bedroom window is no bigger than a postage stamp. My heart is beating recklessly and my hands would be so much better if they had something to hold. I take a breath—the kind that stings the back of your throat—and then I count to ten or twenty or a hundred thousand. Nothing changes. The lights do not flicker. The moon doesn't dip. The sky does not go dark as oil.

I turn around and continue on to the next block and the next, past a row of stores, beyond Ace Hardware, into other neighborhoods where both rambling houses and rattletraps perch at the edge of great lawns, where porchlights shine hot as meteors welcoming somebody home. When finally I don't know where I am anymore, I get smart, as my mother would say. I turn and start back, and at last I'm calm on those sidewalks, I'm limp and light. I watch my feet all the way home, step after step—no melody, no rhythm—until all I know is the beauty of my own shoes.

Evolution of Words

~~~~~~

I tried to see the city as he must have seen it—a miracle of light, the rain-wet streets opening from Battery to Sansome and finally down to Grant. Judd hadn't slept in four nights, and so, when he left his parents' house on the fifth night and walked downtown, the city must have spun with music for him. He was seventeen and sleepless and that close to what his mother would later call "release."

We cried at that. Release. The idea of Judd walking in Chinatown the fifth night, change in his pockets, the on-and-off rain a passage into something we had no knowledge of. He liked it there—Chinatown—the piles of foreign newspapers, the boys with braids, with needletracks dancing up their thin arms. San Francisco was a waking dream that my cousin Judd walked through tirelessly. He didn't want a car. *Leslie Prada and Her Topless Love Act* was something he had to see on foot, next door to The Condor, across from Dutch Boy Paints, and only a half block down from El Cid's *He and She Revue*. "Get a job and you can have a car," Judd's parents told him, but he continued to walk from Nob Hill to Lands' End in tennis shoes and T-shirt, with the long dark hair that would be cut before he was buried. No one knew where my cousin's spending money came from.

For months afterward I looked for answers by trying to re-create the scene of that shadowy fifth night, the world in rags. Even fish sleep, their bodies like silvery, shot arrows lining the Embarcadero and Baker's Beach and spreading outward on waves to Sausalito. Fridays were open buffet at Song Hay, and Judd could have been there that last night, but the restaurant was so busy that the cashier couldn't remember just one boy. An attendant at the Ginn Wall parking lot may have seen Judd, but there was nothing distinctive about my cousin's face, and in the darkness at the corner of the lot a slouching boy in a denim jacket was the least of things to notice. With a Chamber of Commerce city map, I tried to reinvent his path, tracing the cold hard steps he might have taken past the Greyhound Bus Depot and maybe on to the Flower Terminal where the chrysanthemums must have glowed, to him, like an eerie experiment set in white rain. North or south from there, perhaps unable to hitch a ride to Sonoma, cold and breathless and stinging with enough life to ground three people, my cousin turned, wherever he was, and finally headed for the nailhead lights of the Golden Gate Bridge.

That's where I stopped reimagining the scene—the place where Judd put on his Walkman and stepped into air. No one knew how he got past the attendants at the tollbooths. Magic, determination—my cousin wanted to fly, the music pounding in his ears, the rough wind making its momentary promises.

In the gloomy days before the funeral, no one thought about Judd's hair, about the way he had wanted to be. By the time we gave instructions, we were too late. Hyberland's Mortuary had already used army clippers on him.

Judd's mother, entranced, made endless pots of coffee, and it was not until months later that she said it: "release." Sitting at the kitchen table, our hearts turned liquid and we finally caved in.

Now, years later, there are other words we can't get past: "winter," "midnight." Even "water" hits us like a clap of thunder.

A Map of Kansas

〜〜〜〜〜〜〜〜〜〜〜〜〜〜〜〜〜〜〜〜〜〜〜

E arly on a June morning my relatives come driving in from places small and windswept, places with the names of lost souls: Netawaka, Leavenworth, Skiddy, Sabetha. Those who live in the Far West—Liberal or Scott County—have driven through the night or stopped in one of the gray, mid-state, freeway towns where motels raise holy hell with each other in their war for customers. I've seen the signs and come-ons before—Better Queen Sized Beds, Super Satellite Cable, Free Ham and Egg Breakfast—and I've usually been fortunate enough to have somewhere else to stay. A desperate Imperial Inn or Regal 8, say in Salina or Garden City or anywhere in the great slackened palm of mid-Kansas, can signal the beginning of a long and lonely night.

My aunts and uncles and cousins, my half relatives and step-cousins, people who claim to be related to us, and people who belong to our family only by accident or indiscretion—all of them head home for the reunion early on a June morning. They do sixty and seventy miles an hour on the highways, the fields of wheat and sorghum and foot-high corn whipping by in a sweet fast-forward. The rural premise here is to get where you're going. Their windshields fill with the delicate blue and yellow and black of early morning swarms. Almost always there is a baby crying from the back seat and almost always one of my aunts or cousins will turn around from the front seat with a bottle or a Tootsie Pop or a half-serious warning or begin to tiredly open up her blouse. My relatives travel the prairies at the speed of light to get home, maybe to be the first to arrive, maybe to get the long and lonely ride over with—star to star, town to town.

I know long and lonely. I also know joy and comfort and being wanted. My life has taken a wandering path, and maybe I'm smarter because of this. Jean, my mother, thinks we're smarter for having moved to California almost ten years ago, though the day we packed the U-Haul van and left our unfinished basement home in Holton, Kansas, was a hard day, a day with a lot of crying and swearing and promises. I was sixteen then and our leaving for California seemed like a long, interesting part of a movie to me, but my nine-year-old sister Katie was downright scared.

I remember how Jean tried to turn it all into a joke, saying the only way to stop living underground was to move west. "Want to stay in a tomb for the rest of your lives?" she asked us as she carried out a box of Christmas decorations, tinsel and angel hair spilling behind her in a luminescent trail. For twelve years we had lived in the basement of a house whose upper stories, season after season, just never got built. Jean became sick of the dark, dank two-bedroom cigar box, of our sweaters always smelling like pee, and finally she grew tired of Eldon Hyde—a good-enough-looking husband but a poor architect, an idle carpenter, and, worst, a dreamless dreamer. Consequently, Jean drove the U-Haul west, I read the map, and Katie sullenly lost herself in the new Etch-a-Sketch Jean had bribed her with.

In its way, California was good for us. The long, slow, rocky coastline set us free. Soon after we arrived Jean took Katie and me to

Balboa Park and sat us down on a concrete bench in a garden steeped with bird of paradise and zinnias, where the colors rushed in high frequency and the air was glass, and she said, "We're three women now. Comprende vous?"

"We comprende," Katie and I told her, and from then on Jean was Jean to us.

Ten years later, like faithful traveling companions, like people who do not lose each other even after the road, the three of us returned together to the Midwest for the Hillcock reunion. It was June. It was right after Katie completely stopped eating. We came in on a smooth flight, Jean and I tipping a few bourbons, Katie drinking mineral water from a tall plastic container she pulled out of her carry-on tote. Katie had the window seat because, as she put it, she wanted her money's worth.

Katie was worried about money, though that was only indirectly the issue in her life. After two years of studying to become an X-ray technician, she had flunked the test for her certification. "Flat out flunked it," she had said.

"So what? You can take the test again in two months," I told her.

"Look," she said, framed by the bay window in Jean's pink and black ceramic kitchen. "If I don't know the bones yet, if my best X-rays are more like vacation snapshots, then it's over and I'm screwed. Trust me."

"Come on," I said, "you were scared. You blanked. You were temporarily insane the day of the test." But I could see that Katie had already cast those two years into a dismal, untalked-about void that she called her past.

Toward the end of the flight into K.C. International we looked out the cramped porthole, over the wing, and down onto the endless farmland spread like a squared and colorful quilt, as strong in its way as the brown, slave-driven Rockies had been from the air an hour earlier. It's probably true that one place is no better than another. Whatever your location, your heart either pounds with tenderness and love or it fails you. And yet, as I flew over the plains and down into the big, broken wheel of Kansas City I felt better, stronger. I don't know if there are currents in the earth or if some mountains hold power or if certain places pulse with an unknowable energy, but when I finished my third bourbon and unbuckled my seat belt, I felt I was really home.

The last three miles to the Hillcock reunion are on gravel road, and so my relatives slow down just a little, the flying gravel making its own song, dust layering the air brown and then pink. They know the road by heart: the sunlit curves and the soft, sloping shoulders and the old bridges that can spell trouble on a dark-enough night. Fall and winter, this road intimidates, but in summer it falls to its dusty knees, no more than a worn cowpath.

My aunts and uncles and cousins, my half relatives and step-cousins arrive, honking their horns, looking for shade or a level place to park. They drive rusted-out pickups, little dusty Toyotas, one-ton Silverados, and Buick Electras. There's a snub-nosed Ford Falcon next to the mailbox, and some dark-haired kid drives a burnt-out blue Triumph right up to the front porch. "Who is he?" Katie asks me, but I have no idea. He's tall like the Hillcocks, dark-skinned like the Schirmeisters, yet the face has the blonde, softly bearded look of someone outside of memory.

There are at least a handful of people at the reunion whom Katie and I cannot identify. Jean has eight brothers and sisters, all of them here, and they have in turn brought their children and their children's children until the family becomes one of those unruly word problems from math class: how many people does it take to fill a yard starting with one man and one woman who multiply, spring and winter, good times and bad, hit-or-miss, right up into a June morning?

I feel sure that the Hillcocks are a family who, in dire times, could continue to grow on only bread and water and radiant heat. They are

24

not giants. They have worries and fears, sickness and grim crack-ups. Something burns in them, though, low and steady, something that most of them are not even aware of.

My Uncle Samuel, for instance, simply cannot explain how he freed himself from the iron trap of an overturned cultivator. Caught in mud at the end of a row of beets, the big John Deere flipped and pinned him. He says his hands just kept digging for a way out, that he had no strength and that his life was not particularly a tender masterpiece worth saving to him at that moment, but his hands had a will of their own. With a crushed knee and a foot as useless as a flopping trout, he dragged himself halfway to the road, and the last thing he remembered seeing was the big, lilac, blockbuster sky.

On the day of the reunion Katie is already so far gone that the sky means nothing to her. In cutoffs and a denim workshirt, she has taken herself past pretty into the delicate realm of an outline. Food is a quick, efficient link to her life that Katie has cut. Her long, blonde hair lies passively over one shoulder. She moves from cousin to cousin, smiling and wide-eyed, loosening the hold this jagged, green world has on her. Not once have Katie and I actually spoken about what she is doing, and perhaps it is not so much a plan that she has as a place into which she is gradually slipping. The failed test—and I truly believe this—is not the issue for Katie. There is something deeper—a black thread; a twisted, luckless ray of light—that she sees running the length of her life.

"Katie," I have said a million times before, trying to ease the something blue and indistinct in her. "Look out the window," "Bite down hard," "Breathe deeply," "Make a fist," "Color the leaves any goddamn color."

Her response has always been a tired, dreamy look that, if it were not for her lack of acting ability, would represent a cool, haunting Greta Garbo.

Katie is under the big yellow and white canopy that has been borrowed from the Everest United Methodist Church and set up as the shady center of the reunion. She carries her bottle of mineral water—

this in distinct contrast to the ice-cold cans and bottles my relatives carry: Orange Crush, Coke, Budweiser, Coors. The drinking starts at 9 A.M. and proceeds happily, unselfconsciously throughout the day. Twice someone goes into town for more ice. My cousin Bee fills two baby bottles with Coke, then gives them to her eight-month-old twins who sit in their matching high chairs where they are quiet mirror images of themselves. Her twins, six-pound Halloween baby boys, are children numbers six and seven for Bee, who still manages to pour herself into a pair of faded Levis, though there are those of us who wish she wouldn't. To describe Bee as pear-shaped is to misrepresent the pear. Bee's hips spread like hefty parentheses over the sides of the fold-out chairs which have also been borrowed from the Methodists and placed at random under the canopy.

From a moderate distance—say, from the front porch or by the oak tree—it looks as if there is a small, miraculous circus in the yard and my relatives are the awkward knife-throwers and the left-handed magicians. Torn from use, having been folded too many times in the hands of the Ladies Bible Auxiliary, the big top canopy shivers slightly in the breeze like a threadbare tragedy waiting to happen on aluminum poles.

I walk and talk and drink like the best of them, though I cannot say that I really know my relatives. Mostly, we are in a gravitational field where we are pulled together by the idea of a shared name. I suppose there are lesser ideas that have held together poorer people. Day floats overhead, and the wet, penny-colored earth empties itself at our feet—we are that incredibly lucky. Jean says that luck has nothing to do with our lives. "It's guts," she would say, "and stamina and using your good, old noggin," and she would tap her head repeatedly to make her point. But when I think back to the days just before we moved from Kansas I do not particularly see Jean as an example of logic and decorum. I can see her standing in the rototilled yard that my father, Eldon, had decided to make into garden, and with a sweep of her hand she said he could have it all: the blue-black sky and the house that could never get itself up to where a house should be. Jean

26

yelled that all she ever wanted were some windows and a back door that didn't open into a face full of sod.

The basement bedroom where Katie and I slept had begun to show signs of seepage. In the corners and along the floor a coppery water gathered mysteriously. Eldon was in our room every other day with a tube of caulking. That's how I remember my father: blonde, silent, his pockets bulging with putty knives and nails and the tools of what, for him, was a dying art.

I think that even as we loaded the U-Haul Eldon didn't believe we would go. He made one last-ditch effort to keep us. He brought in a load of lumber—some pretty white pine—and stacked it seductively out by the driveway, but we all knew, deep in our hearts, that the wood was destined to warp and turn gray in the seasons when Eldon could not find the right words or locate his good hammer.

The Kansas sky is a lavender wave that extends from your outstretched right hand across countless miles eastward toward the muddy Missouri—the only American river I can never remember being mentioned in a song. It is not necessarily a kind sky. I have seen the brooding tails of tornadoes slip down from the clouds and rip northerly through Sedgwick and Lyon and Shawnee counties. I have watched Perry Reservoir shrink and harden into a wasp nest when the sky glazed over in late summer. But a sky like this at least tends to remind you who you are.

On that June day we are the painstaking makers of a party where ice quickly becomes the most valuable commodity. Four styrofoam ice chests and three cooling watermelons make their demands. Then, too, the kids have organized a touch-and-go ice war which lasts until Serina, a six-year-old beauty belonging to one of my cousins, takes a cold, hard hit on the cheekbone. Serina cries and swears she's going to die, but her mother holds her and tells her that it's not that easy.

Sitting under the canopy, dressed in the blue workshirt that bares the pale *T* of her throat and upper chest, Katie, I think, would agree—she is taking the long, hard way out. Her shoulders, somewhere beneath that oversized shirt, have lately assumed the resemblance of handlebars.

"Close your eyes," I have told her a hundred, a thousand times before. "Let it go," "Make a wish," "Turn up the radio," but my advice has only been helpless, broad strokes.

I don't know what burdens we carry, why some of us are stranded on high ground and others simply washed away. I have looked for the answers, though, and I have spared no expense. For almost two years I paid Rhea Blanco, an overpriced therapist in La Jolla, to uncover what she said were my layers of blocking and denial. She sat me down in a leather chair and had me look at driftwood. I told her that I had been in and out of six serious relationships in the past three years, some of them occurring at the same time, and before that, there was a whole string of men and boys whom I validly cared for but could not, inevitably, stay with. Among other things, Rhea told me that I hated my father and that was why I could not be content with any man.

Later Werner Kausman, a rolfing specialist and part-time primal rebirther, suggested that I loved Eldon far too much and that these feelings had thrown me out of balance. Werner had this great shock of white hair and huge, expressive hands, and one afternoon we started kissing in his office. Putting on my lipstick before I left that day, I asked him if he was going to charge me for an office visit or for a full-blown consultation. He didn't think that was funny.

It was Rosaline D'Ametri, the owner of Rosa's Shrimp and Chips, who sat me down at her counter which overlooked the Crystal Pier and told me not to worry, that one man is simply not enough for a woman. "Maybe some day you settle for one," she said, "but right now . . ." She shook her head and patted my hand. We looked dreamily out the window together, into light fog and what passes for a sky in southern California.

In Kansas there are no leaps of faith necessary when you look up—the sky veers suddenly into your path, deep and unavoidable. Sometimes it is a low, dark roof over your head, and at other times it is high-strung and electric.

On the day of the reunion there is a sense that the sky is about to fall, that the wavy horizon is the not-so-distant edge where things begin to crumble. My sister's eyes are hungry and bright, and her long, straight hair recalls both pleasure and beauty. My relatives don't know her well enough to see what is happening. They think of her as thin and distant. Even Jean successfully ignores what she probably couldn't do anything about. It seems like a long time ago—Balboa Park or the wet, marbled stretch of some beach—when Jean handed Katie over to me, just relinquished the best, most beautiful thing in her life without a word.

On an early June morning Katie and I watch my relatives pack in the food that will feed not only us, but all the 4-H'ers on this side of the scrub-oaked Missouri bluffs. I watch with polite anticipation while Katie watches with something more akin to dread. All of the food is in Tupperware or under double layers of plastic wrap. Some of the food is cut into chunky, fist-sized pieces. The milk gravy is ladled with a coffee mug, and the big, broad serving spoons on the table suggest appetites that are beyond the body's simple needs. In cake pans and chipped brown crockery, their food is a reckless affirmation of here and now.

When it's time to eat, someone says a short, quick prayer so that the major operating principle of the day won't be compromised: hot food hot and cold food cold. We are people who are headstrong and in love with the world when we have paper plates in our hands. We can work a two-sided buffet line with a snap of our fingers. We have homing devices that can take us within inches of where the desserts are being hidden—the cherry pie with the sugared crust, the punch-and-pour chocolate cake. I take Katie a slice of banana bread and two brownies. "Let's see," she says when I put them in front of her, "would it be animal, vegetable, or mineral?" Any answer I give would not interest her, though.

After the meal there is a lull under the yellow and white canopy.

Bee's twins are asleep in their high chairs, cracker crumbs spread in a three-foot circle around them. Their bald heads fall to their chests like sprung toys, and I ask Bee if we should take the boys into my grandparents' house and lay a blanket on the floor for them.

"Oh no," she says. "They like to sleep like that."

As if in response, the breeze quickens and the huge trees—the oaks and the cottonwoods—stir with the softness of nets being cast. It is an old, cool wind that blows in off the Missouri, south through the Lansing orchards, and over the silent, seminal fields of wheat. It is a wind that carries the voices of the Hillcock children who are in the green and sunflowered pasture where only Pig Latin is allowed. Then, too, it is a wind that spirals up a thick, sweet smell from the storm cellar—a little homegrown that burns quick as rope and eases the teenaged boys into the afternoon. For them, the skating rink in Centralia has become boring. The shopping mall in Manhattan is no fun since they can't drop snow cones onto the shoppers below anymore. For them, Kansas is the cold, dead center of an otherwise teeming world, but I could tell them differently. I could say that the miles of openness—green and gold and quaking silver—might be closer to reality than anywhere else they could drive; that in the seven miles between Circleville and Fostoria there is more meaning than in the entire Rose Bowl Parade.

Sometime past two or three o'clock—I don't know; time tapers and descends in those afternoons—the traditional softball game is started. We have no gloves and the ball is rock-hard and lopsided from being left out in the rain, but if spirit counts for anything, we are rich and well supplied. The bases are marked by rags held down with rocks, but the overgrown grass in the pasture where we play makes the bases impossible to see, and so we end up simply running for each other—toward the first and second and third basemen, whoever they are. Once in a while someone hits the ball senseless, and then time flies as we formally search the grass for the ball—a dingy, white speck in a storyteller's green ocean.

My relatives do not make spectacular catches, and in the outfield they appear as shy, bighearted people among the goldenrod. Whoever steps up to bat is a good-for-nothing, a nearsighted dog, a puny traitor from the other side. The pitches range from halfhearted spitballs to loop-the-loops. Everyone gets a chance to knock the ball to hell, but mostly we tap it to the shortstop.

My aunts and uncles and cousins are big, loose people. They run the bases, always looking forward. Their thick hair shines like a lesson in light, and when they bend to pick up the ball or merely to scratch their feet there is no misery or misfortune in the world.

I like to think of the rest of that June day as the softball game. I like to imagine all of us—connected by blood or name or something even less tangible—in a pasture bordered by a creek that eventually runs past Meriden and Valley Falls and the Kickapoo Indian Reservation and empties into the dark, bridgeless Nemeha.

In actuality, the day does not end in the pasture. It proceeds onto the porch and into the kitchen. There are those who gather in the living room to watch the six o'clock news, and in the front yard someone's gallbladder operation is being retold with amazing detail and authenticity.

My relatives do not give up a ship easily. They stay past dark, sometimes past their welcome. Their children are inventive and find games to play in closets and parked cars, at the side of the house, and in the rubble around the toolshed.

When my relatives clear a table for the night, they do so carefully. They cover the food and wipe the table down. They leave the sugar bowl out, and fill the salt and pepper. Each small act is a gesture of confidence that there will absolutely be a tomorrow and tomorrow.

In Kansas the night surrounds a house; it does not swallow the house, it does not turn the house to stone starting from the inside out, as sometimes happens in California. You can think of the Kansas night as a hand covering a flame. You can imagine the dusk as a fine, dark cloth being laid in a line over Mayetta and west toward Wamego and farther west toward Abilene and Great Bend.

Though it is a sweeping, dramatic darkness, it is not black. In fact,

I can see Katie sitting in the dark under the yellow and white canopy and I can already make out the strong line of her jaw and her thin, hairpin wrists. Like Katie, I am unable to properly name these bones.

In Kansas in the dark, my sister is all softness and memory as she sits there rehearsing the silence that will steadily grow around her. Katie—the riddle of woods, the renderless garden. Not far away, I am looking at her, thinking of her. I am listening to the crickets shape and reshape this fierce world.

Chocolate

I remember a birthday when there was hardly anything for me—a pair of blue mittens wrapped in a Husted's Dry Cleaning sack, brown twine tied in a lopsided bow around it all. With her eyebrow pencil, Libby, my mother, had written on the package: To Janice, Our Angel. I sat with my arms folded and refused to move. I didn't want to turn nine that year in the dull, beat-up world of Idaho and welfare.

Besides pretending that it was ribbon fit for an angel, Libby used the brown twine to secure the lampshade on the lamp and also to tie the back door shut, which had no lock. "You want the whole world coming in?" she'd ask, her small chapped hands struggling to tie a box knot over the doorknob, but in fact, if burglars had ever come to our house, they would have looked around, pulled the stocking caps off their faces, and laughed. A chenille bedspread at our front window for drapes. An empty orange crate painted red as an end table.

I was miserable when my mother laid that birthday package on the table, the dry cleaning label face-up and taunting me, but then my father, Noel, arrived with chocolate. Not a box, but a sack with the assorted specialties from Selfaggio's—Twin Falls' best gift and confection shop, though Noel always said it "gift and affection."

We did not talk. We sat back with chocolate melting on our tongues and fell into the sugary comas that often mark the lives of the poor. My little sisters folded their hands in their laps and swung their feet—scuffed saddle shoes, penny loafers with the stitching popped, high-topped leather baby boots not fit for learning the art of walking in. Despite our outward circumstances, my parents believed that we were cultured, in a sense—could distinguish German from Swiss choco-late, a good hazelnut from a bad. They taught us how to savor, how to close our eyes and be romanced in the thick language of taste.

Later that night I opened my gift. "Next year," Libby said to Noel for my benefit, "don't you think Janice will be ready for a bike next year?" For me, it was not that dangling promise which never came true, but the dark, rivery liqueur centers of the candy that made nine seem possible and, at least for a moment, even good.

My past, in the most simple terms, was a series of awkward, shame-ful gifts, starting with those mittens, starting when the Twin Falls Mill closed and my parents discovered that they liked the shabby life of leisure. One year there was a pair of men's scruffy, used downhill skiis for me. I never got boots or poles to go with them, was never once taken to a ski resort. Noel, I later learned, had taken them as payment on a bet he'd won. At first he refused them, but then remembered that my birthday had passed uneventfully two days before, so he loaded them in the junkpile Pinto he drove.

In Idaho on welfare, skiing lessons were not possible; ballet classes were totally out of the question. There was black and white TV if the electricity had been paid. There was a deck of cards with naked women on the backs which could be used if Libby was not enrapt in solitaire. And, of course, from time to time there was chocolate.

One year it came from Ghiardelli's, shipped to us in a discreet brown package, the chocolate wrapped in soft insulated foil. It was a five-pound block, and Noel slowly unwrapped it much like I thought other fathers might unwrap a bowling trophy or a beautiful Father's Day tie. By slivers, we ate that block of chocolate, tasting how the bitter and the sweet were suspended together, which was the lesson of life in windy Idaho, where the snow or the dust was always blowing—either "salt or pepper," we always said.

I remember not wanting to turn eleven, not wanting to turn twelve, and then not wanting Christmas. Under the tree there was a huge toad in a cracked glass aquarium for my sister Marnie. She was six and terrified of the dazed thing that kept jumping against the glass until it finally and forever lay still. A used crock pot for Libby that had the faint odor of someone's burned chili still in it. We maneuvered through that Christmas and its gifts like, I suppose, you tiptoe through land mines. Relief and wet underarms when it was all through.

The impossible darkness of turning sixteen took hold of me, and honestly I can't say what it was that birthday that Libby and Noel dreamed up: a garage-sale coat, somebody's worn-out flute with a six-pack of loose sheet music which, of course, I wouldn't have been able to read. By then I was so full of wanting that I couldn't see straight.

It took the next twenty years to get beyond all that. Cordell Murphy, my husband, paid for me to forget. Massage, long afternoons of counseling, three weeks in the Alps in total silence. Finally discouraged with my slow progress, he took me to the side of our house one Fourth of July and hit my head twice against the shake shingles. I kicked back and then it was over—the foul taste of powdered milk. My irrational yearning for silk, for trinkets, for shoes, for socks. The gruesome details of chocolate.

Paperweight

If it weren't for my body, I could fly, I could go anywhere, I could be anything. I learned this fact long ago, and yes, there was regret and suffering from it, there were nights I cried, there were whole summers spent in an upstairs bedroom where I surrounded myself with ladies' magazines and poetry and my brother's borrowed *Penthouse*. Lying across the bed or spread on the parquet floor, I was the tall, sad witness to myself: arms and legs and all the rest of me that I wouldn't have given fifty cents for.

When I think of my body, I usually see Martin Heffler trying to pull open the stage curtains for our fifth grade's rendition of *How the West Was Won*. Martin was only a fourth grader, and maybe that had something to do with it, but really, it was the curtains that wouldn't budge—gold brocaded velvet, beautiful to look at, but ponderous as a ton of wet laundry. At the far right of the stage Martin was up there grunting, actually grunting. He was red-faced and the curtains

36

weren't going anywhere. Cruelty, inattention—I don't know what it was, but the teachers just let poor Martin struggle for a while, which was wrong because they basically understood the laws of physics. The curtains were a rock and Martin was a pebble.

How the West Was Won turned out to be more an assignment than an artistic creation. The pioneers were deadpan and the Indians communicated only with timid war whoops. By far, it was Martin Heffler who had stolen the show and lent me this image of my body as something heavier than night and beyond the laws of physics: the cumbersome gold curtains behind which Emily Mills, dressed as the state of California, waited to be discovered.

It goes back that far, to grade school, to Martin raging against those curtains and me sitting in the audience with the first realization of being trapped head-on, my body a hopeless house with the doors all locked. I wasn't sure at the end of the play if I could stand up. I felt as if I had melted into my chair. The fourth graders were all shuffling around me, and the big sixth graders seemed awkward and pinned in their clothes.

That was the start of a physical disorientation that would visit my life again and again. One night in St. Louis in 1976, Prentice Dorn left his post at the bar and delivered his body to me, tall and dark-haired, a man whose hands are more committed to my memory than his face, not because he was unattractive, but simply that his hands moved so smoothly. They were like water as it edges around something big, as it pools and cuts until everything is surrendered without a sound.

Prentice had already finished cleaning the bar and was following me around. It was after closing and I'd only had the job at Fiddler's for three weeks. Prentice had worked there for over two years. He was telling me how Walter, the maître d', had fouled up some reservations that evening and how a furious party of six had been left sitting in the lobby for over a half hour. Walter had given them a round of complimentary cocktails and humbled himself in a slew of perfected apologies, then taken it all out on the two nearest waiters. And if Nick was too stupid to notice that the busboys were stealing his tips, Prentice maintained, then he deserved it.

This was stuff I liked to hear about, everything I couldn't see from the kitchen, though I didn't envy those who worked the dining room, who stepped lightly among the tables of St. Louis socialites in the half-dark elegance that was as imagined as real. A waterfall of blue-green lights, potted fig trees and magnolias—it was a strange place to work, an old establishment that soothed and charmed the public. There was constant bickering among the cooks—what could be served with what, who threw out the last can of peppercorns. Back by the coffee station, the busboys hung out and watched the plates as they were taken from tables. Leftovers were up for grabs, the good stuff: the practically untouched prime rib or lobster or the Wellington. Nobody went away from this place hungry. John, one of the waiters, would leave quietly after midnight with cake or eclairs for his little girls. Even the cats survived by prowling the garbage cans out back. It was the way that city fed itself, and no one thought of it as stealing.

I knew, as he followed me into the pantry and back out to the prep station, that Prentice was sizing me up. He had watched me like this for three nights, following me out to my car where he stood complicating the darkness, talking about St. Louis's water system and his father's bowling alley and a host of trivia that, though meaningless to me, was tender.

So on this the fourth night, when I reached up to slide a five-pound can of olives onto the shelf and felt Prentice close behind me, his arms around my waist, I was not surprised. In fact, I leaned into him the way a person leans into a storm, a little off balance perhaps, but determined to keep going, despite the wind and the rain. It was an awkward moment, Prentice kissing my hair because he couldn't get to my face. I couldn't get to anything on Prentice, so I leaned back farther into his arms, into his chest, to the place where his heart became the same pounding as Walter's fist on the outside door. He had locked himself out and wanted to know why it took so long for us to get there.

That was the fourth night, April, when Prentice took two bottles of the house Zinfandel and we left Fiddler's, though we were unable to make it all the way up the stairs to his apartment. We had to stop out there on his porch to taste each other, mouth and neck and shoulders, everything unwinding into the black shoal of night that is St. Louis in summer. If I could, this is where I would have stopped it, on the porch where desire was still blind, where it was only a sound—the whining first gear of a car or dogs barking in the distance. But Prentice unlocked the door, he opened the wine with a deep, resounding pop, and the next eight years began to take shape.

Later that night in Prentice's bed I started at his foot and dreamed my way up his leg in the old way, like the pioneers scratching at the dirt, looking for signs, for smoke, for California. Prentice moaned a little. It was the kind of sound that's hard to distinguish. Sometimes it's pain; sometimes it's heaven and there's no word, there's just this sound that comes out into the room, all breath and feeling. Side by side, caught on warm sheets, our arms were too heavy to let each other go.

"Do you want coffee?" Prentice asked me in the morning.

"Yeah. Always," I told him.

It wasn't a test, though to watch a man moving around in his own kitchen is a kind of revelation. Prentice had a specific cabinet for cups. Things were looking good.

Prentice in the morning in his boxer shorts. Why is the world that kind of place, happiness and sadness converging, the smell of coffee making everything new?

———~~~~~~~~———

There is a moment when I look down at myself and the consequences of life are made real. Ankle and skin and bone, the long curve of the arm, a patch of hair. When I step from the shower, my skin sings and there is nothing I can do about it.

With clay, you get to feel what the body is really like. I'm just a part-time sculptor, but even I know that the hands are incredible. There are twenty-seven bones in them, and then the wrists turn in, delicate as stems, frustrating you, making you cry. Once I worked on a foot for a whole month. I made all my visitors take off their shoes when they came into the house so I could study their feet, and still my foot, if I had to tell the truth, was mediocre. At Christmas, as a joke, I sculpted Allen's balls, but they cracked when I fired them. They're on my desk now, paperweights, a sad reminder of Allen, my first love, at the AmTrak station when I gave him two apples and a box of Jujubes and told him that love shouldn't feel like despair. Dressed in coats and mufflers, our hands feeling old but unprepared, we said good-bye, waving for what seemed like hours.

～～～～～～～

Fiddler's wasn't four stars, but it definitely had a reputation. The service was good, the food hot, and the frilly garnishes oftentimes breathtaking. Even though Walter had lived in St. Louis for over twenty years, he played up his Algerian accent, and the customers were delighted. In the safe confines of the kitchen, though, he returned to his everyday slang, to name-calling and cracking the whip, to pointing out that all busboys were born with their heads up their asses.

From six until ten I was a slave, then the dinner rush died, I got myself a drink and started cleanup. The front doors were locked at twelve and on good nights I was out of there by one.

Theft is a harsh word, but it's the word Ron Mayfield used when he spoke to the night shift one Friday before we went to work. Even though he was one of the owners, we didn't see him that often because he lived in Frankfort, so when he walked in, his gray Saab parked in the loading zone, we stiffened a little, and Nick, who was about to throw a loaf of French bread rocket-style across the room and onto the counter, gracefully put his arm down and strode across the kitchen like, hey, it was just work as usual.

Mayfield had a way of making it seem all very vague: inventories and loss statements. He avoided being accusatory. If I had been a jury and looked out into their faces, I wouldn't have seen anything, not from the cooks or the busboys or the waiters or anybody. Simply put: nobody here had stolen a thing. Mayfield was having a business problem; that's what it was, and maybe we even sympathized with him a little.

Nothing really changed. Oh, one night Walter saw John leaving with a couple of slices of raspberry torte, and he told John to put them in take-out containers, but that was it.

I told Prentice, who was still wiping down the bar when John left, what Walter had done.

"Yeah, he's O.K.," Prentice said.

I sat down on one of the stools. The lights in the dining room behind us were already out, and for some reason Prentice was moving slowly that night, taking his time with the glasses and carefully folding every dishrag. In another month he was due to start an internship with a local architect and he planned to cut down on his hours at the restaurant then. I had been thinking of that, of the fact that I would be seeing him less.

Prentice was beautiful at his work. No, he was beautiful doing anything. I saw him mowing his father's yard once. He had to stop and empty the grass catcher every couple of times around the yard. His shirt was off and the air was sweet with St. Augustine and there seemed nothing better than this small, raw world. His father came out on the porch and I could see the resemblance and I thought: whatever happens, I'll be better for this.

"Prentice," I said, bending a straw in half, "do you think it's stealing?" It wasn't a test; it was a question, though I admit there was a lot in it. Prentice covered a bowl of cut limes and looked up at me. He was tired, he was running late, but he paused thoughtfully and then he said, "Dee, everything is stealing."

~~~~~~~~~

It was a really bad year for Martin Heffler—a year of bad luck and misunderstanding and letting the hammer fall. Besides the humiliation suffered in those few minutes before Mrs. Gallagher's sixth graders claimed the West, Martin underwent the trauma of being accused of stealing. Birdy Watson, a melancholic redhead who clung to the cyclone fence at recess, stood up just before lunch and yelled that his lunch ticket was gone, and several other students discovered theirs missing also. Through a long process that involved a desk search, conferences, an anonymous note, and a lecture on the importance of truth and honor, Martin's name was arrived at. No formal punishment was dealt out as far as we knew, but Martin was a small boy, and if anything, he lost weight that year. He took to folding his homework into tiny squares the size of quarters, and later on he stopped riding the bus.

So when Prentice told me that everything was stealing, I remembered Martin and the Zinfandel and Walter turning his head and the cats slinking up the alley. I saw Allen with the apples and my heart, and I saw myself turning to Prentice in the night, throwing the covers back and easing onto him, telling him there and there.

The most I ever took from Fiddler's was a cherry cream pie. I was having lunch guests the next day and Estelle, the pastry chef, said to go ahead, in another day or so it was going to be stale anyway. It was a whole pie, eight pieces, with crème de glace and everything. I served it on these little bone china plates, and all I had were salad forks, but I used them and it didn't matter.

Prentice was even less a thief than I. On occasion he helped himself to what he wanted, but this was excusable because he was never paid for all the work he did. Constantly he'd be in there on his day off or before his shift. In an emergency, Prentice was always there, like when the pipes burst or when they needed someone to pick up new kitchen equipment from Cleveland.

Prentice was a real asset. Prentice was the man who bought me three rings and moved me twice. After his internship with Signature One Consultants, they hired him full time, and then he only came into Fiddler's with clients or sometimes alone for a nightcap.

"Prentice, are you happy?" I asked him.

"Happy," he answered, but it was the kind of response I could never trust.

I told him to explain, that there were all kinds of happy, that we should know each other's mind.

"O.K.," he said, pretending concentration, eyes closed tight, hand on his forehead. "Tell me what I'm thinking."

What I'm thinking is that you can never leave a body until the very end, like that moment in Ripley's Believe It or Not when they show a man and his body finally separating from each other. It's an old photograph and the authenticity is questionable, but the idea itself is wonderful, how you get up and walk across the room and just leave your body lying there.

It's not bitterness that makes me say this. It's simply how much my body possesses me, how Prentice would stand in a doorway and I'd be unable to think clearly. In the mornings, how the warm sunlight could tie me to the ground or how I could shiver and ache—almost like the flu—for one good kiss.

One night I thought I lost my body in the main branch of the St. Louis Public Library, but if so, it hadn't gone far. I'd been reading an oversized reference book, Twelve Moons of the Year, and it was closing time, and when I stood to leave I was thinking of the final illustration in the book—a landscape, winter-brilliant, the stars caught in the high, barren treetops. It wasn't until I was in my car and five blocks away that I looked down, and like a tired swimmer come back to the shore, it was there, all of it, my knees and breasts and the small of my back, which later that night Prentice moved to and kissed twice: once cold and light, then a second that lingered.

———————

I gave up doing hair and there was only one kind of eyebrow I was any good at. Prentice came in and saw the mess, saw my face smeared with dried clay and just smiled.

"No, I can't get studio space at the junior college," I told him.

"I didn't say anything. Relax." And he made his way to the kitchen.

In '80 we went to Minneapolis to visit his mother and a couple of years after that we camped in the Ozarks, which later Prentice admitted was not all that restful as a vacation. The trails were poor and the season unusually wet.

From the other side of the room, Prentice watched me so often. What he saw was probably no different than clay: an impasse, a collarbone. The small features of children that, when set in marble, seem no more than strokes or petals. His hands knew these things as well as mine.

The best present that I ever gave Prentice was on the occasion of his going-away party from Fiddler's. He was kind of embarrassed with everyone standing around in the lounge in their street clothes, but he appeared cool and gracious nonetheless. I let him open the gift in the car, and he was surprised, if not also confused. It was a three-foot porcelain platter shaped like a fish. The scales were in detail, shimmering, and the eye, an oval of gold leaf. I had found it in an Oriental market, and the only time Prentice took it off his coffee table was the Thanksgiving we tried to serve the turkey on it, but it was all wrong. Prentice was always slightly overwhelmed with gifts. He'd look at them closely, amazed, and he'd thank you ten times.

When I think of my body next to Prentice, I see how time is a ritual, a complicated working out of who will reach over and turn the lamp off at night, of how things will finally be said and done.

"Dee, it's not too late for med school," my mother offered long-distance from Boulder, but Prentice and I were still together. She had no idea what it was like, this body, walking downtown and smelling rain, to be taut and wingless and waiting in a crowd for the bus with this bag of tricks, with this body, with wet hair.

St. Louis is an old place, but it had attempted to modernize itself. There was a pretty successful renovation project downtown, though there were still the rattraps and walk-ups that could be had cheap. It was a city that didn't demand much. It could be traversed easily, the neighborhood sidewalks were wide, and its economy was moderate but growing. I wouldn't consider going back there, though it's a place that I'm glad I lived in for a while.

In St. Louis on my thirtieth birthday Prentice gave me a ring, a garnet: a black-red stone set in a gold band. I couldn't ask him what it meant. Anyway, what could he have said? There were twenty-seven bones in Prentice's hand when he touched me, when he laid back the flesh, there and there, and found only a sparrow's black-red heart.

~~~~~~~~~~

After all of that, after eight years in St. Louis, I ended up going to Boulder, though I warned my mother that medical school was out. No questions. I took my time getting there: three days during which I often stopped to read the map, checking the way Interstate 40 bull-dozed through Illinois and Missouri and Kansas, then, outside of Denver, how it burst into spider lines going everywhere. On the third day I had to stop to repack something I'd hastily arranged in the back seat. The ironing board was hitting the TV screen every time I braked. It was just past Salina, a rest stop from which the great American prairie rolled westward, not exactly as the fifth graders had made it out to be, but lonely all the same. The wind was blowing as it usually does there, cool and unpredictable. If you could have stood there by my car and felt it, you'd know why California is such a happy place and why the settlers cried into the soil, feeling the full weight of their bodies.

In the Shadows of Upshot-Knothole

$\sim\sim\sim\sim\sim\sim\sim\sim\sim\sim\sim\sim\sim\sim\sim\sim\sim\sim$

My mother and I ran away only one time, on a sunny May morning when the world was about to end. She didn't know where we were running to, but my mother Lorraine was smart and she would have figured something out, a place for us to go—Cedar City or Tonopah. For a while after she met my father and married him, my mother said that she only thought between her legs, but time had passed and I'd come along and life had resumed its normal colors and she was trying to think with her head again. Lewis and Elly Barlow, our nearest neighbors, lived almost four miles away on a dirt road that cut through sagebrush and scruffy cedar, and since my mother was on foot and I was in a stroller, their house was the first stop on our way to somewhere, to any place without movie stars.

We had left my father back at the house sitting sullenly on a kitchen chair, and even then he looked a little too much like Tony Curtis to my mother's way of thinking. Black slick hair, a face that you remembered as cheekbones and clear eyes. He was all shoulders and tight waist and he had a raw sleepy sexiness that he knew nothing about. That morning, though, his arms were folded over his chest and he sat in the chair tipped back on its two legs and he was staring at the wall, tired and angry. He said my mother didn't understand him.

The breakfast dishes had just been washed—cups and bowls and plates stacked into the small artful piles that women can make of ordinary things. My mother had dried her hands, stepped over me on the floor where I had balled the rug up around me, and gone to my father's side. "This is what I understand," she said, her voice rising, straining, finally sending Lowry, our big nearsighted collie, slinking from the room. "You'd rather go off and play than stay here with your wife and daughter."

My father had no response to that—sometimes he was tongue-tied; sometimes he needed to filter things and kick some dirt before clarity rushed him—but it didn't matter because my mother spun around, walked back to the bedroom, and began to collect the odds and ends that would compose our survival kit: a hairbrush, a silver baby spoon, a Sears and Roebuck catalog, talcum powder, an eyebrow pencil, diapers. She threw them into a water-stained overnight case and she did it loudly so that my father could hear in the next room, but he didn't budge. They were at one of those impasses where husbands and wives sometimes find themselves—exhausted, speechless, the reckless fear that things will never be the same growing larger and more distinct by the second.

My mother didn't say good-bye. She just walked out into the kitchen with me on her hip and we stood there like a last photograph for my father. He never looked away from the green and white wall-paper checks on the kitchen wall. I drooled and gurgled and reached for him, my mother tells me, my hands round and fat as little pincushions, but he didn't move. He had a point to make and he was serious about it, the chair tipped back, his silence stretching beyond the movies, beyond all the dark-haired leading men into our early morning reality.

My mother was in every way his match. She gathered our things like the slender tornado she could be. Gracefully she walked down the front steps of the house with all the future she could carry—me and an overloaded suitcase and a wobbly baby stroller—and when we were out in the yard she put the suitcase down, wrestled the stroller with one hand, locked the legs into place, and slipped me in.

I was a year old, just a small flowing river of sounds, words that spun unrecognizable, but my mother and I had complete conversations anyway. She says that she had been waiting her whole life for me. When I arrived, there was a lot for us to talk about.

With the suitcase in one hand and the stroller handle in the other, she pushed and explained. "Everything is going to be all right, sweetheart. These things just happen. Your dad has some silly idea stuck in his head and he can't get rid of it."

I reached up with one hand and batted the endless blue sky and jabbered a hundred things back to my mother, and she listened and sorted it out and understood.

"I know. I know," she said. "He's immature. More looks than brains."

I took hold of the plastic stroller tray in front of me and shook it and it seemed to be just the advice my mother was looking for.

"You're right," she said. "I've gone weak and one-minded every time he turned those big blues on me. Putty in his hands. But no more. It's time to get things rolling." As if it were a pact we were keeping, she stopped and reached down and touched my head—a mass of curls that kept me prisoner until I was old enough to find the scissors and cut it myself. "Okay," she said, "it's agreed upon, love pie," and when she started pushing the stroller again, the wheels went straighter and we moved faster, though on a rutted dirt road that even the county wouldn't claim there was no such thing as speed.

Months before I was born, my mother had mail-ordered that stroller and x'ed off the days on Hinkley's Feed and Grain calendar until it arrived. "You won't be able to use it out here," my father had told her, but my mother was determined to do things right, to push me in a stroller like any other baby, despite the fact that the nearest sidewalk or park was a rough forty miles away. She used to tell people that we lived an hour and a half from nowhere, on a rocky ranch headed for no good, and she was just about right. In the southwest corner of Utah, amidst backcountry that was hallucinogenic in its loneliness and landscape, my father's family had slowly carved out a ranch.

The stroller proved difficult but not unmanageable out there, though my mother that morning had only one hand to use. When the wheels stopped in the ruts or hit loose dirt, she placed her hip against the handle, pushed hard with all of her one hundred and fifteen pounds, and got us moving again.

Who can really know the exact moment when something begins, but my mother's opinion is that the real trouble with my father had started months before when Milo de Rossi's car drove up, dust flying, the horn honking, two girls in the back seat tangled up with de Rossi in a way that was still illegal in this state. He introduced the girls as actresses.

Later my mother looked at my father and scowled and, because her hands were full of wet laundry, blew a piece of hair tiredly away from her forehead. "Warren," she said, "let me ask you this. How many movies do you think those girls have been in?"

He stuck his hand in his back pocket, as if to get more room for thinking, and before he could answer she continued. "Looks like they got the auditioning down."

Milo de Rossi had been looking for a place to film his next movie and he'd heard about our ranch and the land it sat on: red cliffs, deep canyons, and the stark Bull Mountains in the distance. He found our land to be a cheap and ready-made set, just as other producers discovered it and made it fit their needs. With a few props and the right camera angles, our ranch was alternately transformed during the early 50's into the Sahara, the moon, the Apache nation, and a hidden Mexican outpost filled with copper-faced desperados. In one of the lowest budget films ever, my father watched cavemen battle dinosaurs in the mock prehistoric valley just below our house, and everything in those ten days of filming would have been perfect had my father not got into a shoving match with a caveman who, during a break, flirtingly lifted the edge of my mother's skirt with his spear and then grunted.

Milo de Rossi was not the first director to visit us, to shake my father's hand and make a deal, but he was the first to tempt him. "And by the way," he had said to him casually, "we might be able to use you in a few scenes that haven't been fully written yet." De Rossi backed up, squared his hands out in front of his face to make a fleshy lens through which to look my father over. "Turn to the left, Warren, and lift your chin a little." My father complied, looking straight into the sun, squinting in a way that would later become Clint Eastwood's seering trademark.

They say that acting is a bug that bites, and if that's true, then my mother could tell you how that bite makes a person sick. My father didn't run a fever after de Rossi left, but he was as hot and irrational as a child with the flu.

"Honey," my mother tried to tell him, "the movies are a long shot. And you can't trust those people."

But my father had taken up staring at the horizon. He rode his horse and irrigated and cut hay and worked hard like he always did, though de Rossi had planted a tantalizing idea out in front of him. And around that time my mother noticed how often he was combing his hair. Any reflective surface would do: a fender, a piece of glass, the still surface of water. By then de Rossi and his crew were due back in three weeks.

We didn't wait for bad news to collapse around us. When my father had turned ice cold that morning and said that his mind was made up, that he'd take whatever de Rossi would give him and that he'd work his way up from there, my mother set her shoulders, let him have one last look at us, and headed out.

The sun was warm and she had stopped to give me a bottle of water. "Hey sweet meat, we're doing fine," she said, kissed both my arms, tickled the warm wet spot under my chin, and pushed the stroller on. The breeze quickened and the cedars waved. A sugar-fine pelting of dust blew over my mother's ankles and between the stroller wheels, and from some indeterminate distance we heard a cow bellowing, low and sorrowful, then echoing back to itself off the high sandstone cliffs.

~~~~~~~~~~

Some said the sky turned liquid; others, that it flexed and burned like at the beginning of time, but what we had seen from our ranch many times before were sudden long flashes as if a huge brilliant light had been turned on and then off in the distance. Ninety-eight miles away as the birds fly was the Nevada Test Site and in the middle of that was Yucca Flat, ground zero. From hillsides on our property we had watched the explosions of test bombs Ruth, Dixie, Ray, Badger, and Simon. Sometimes we packed fruit or a small picnic to take along, we threw an old blanket on the ground, stretched out and waited, but we had grown bored with those events, stopped watching, and accepted the bulletins which said everything was safe.

That morning, predawn, 1953, as part of the series of bombs code-named Upshot-Knothole, Harry had been detonated, a shot that was named to sound as if you were talking about a friendly next-door neighbor. It hung from a 300-foot steel tower out there on Yucca Flat. At the end of the countdown, soldiers positioned three miles away as firsthand observers heard a loud click and then felt the raving heat of a new sun. They had been ordered down on one knee, left arms tight over their closed eyes, heads tucked. In those first two seconds of Harry, some of them saw the bones in their own arms—everywhere a huge luminous X-ray spreading outward. The ground shook and then the shock wave hit, knocking some of the men back, a wave that they eerily felt pass right through their bodies, front to back. And then the sound.

Some soldiers put their hands over their ears, though they had been instructed to keep their eyes covered. Others held their heads against the intense pressure of the blast. They felt a sudden heat in places like their kneecaps and the backs of their hands, and a slow—almost pleasant—tingling in their crotches that shortly, however, turned to painful needling. A private first class jumped up, hollering, holding himself between his legs, but a buddy pulled him back down where he crouched and covered his head and moaned.

Little by little the roaring diminished and the soldiers' heads came up. They uncovered their ears and were ordered to stand. By that time darkness was ebbing and against the mauve sky they saw a swirling golden fireball, alive, kinetic. The gaseous ring around it shimmered red, green, and blue and even the most nervous and frightened soldiers saw it as beautiful, mesmerizing. They watched as the fireball was lifted higher and higher in a mass of roiling gray-black clouds, which didn't mushroom as they usually did, but spread and then drifted.

A sergeant yelled for the men to double-time it into nearby assault vehicles, and when loaded, they headed for ground zero. They drove past a line of mannequins that had been planted upright on metal poles. The mannequins had been suited up in utility jackets and helmets and then placed in formation like a scraggly half-wit battalion. The helmets had been blown off, the jackets were burning, and the mannequin faces had melted into flesh-colored pools onto the desert floor. The vehicles slowed. Some of the soldiers laughed as they went by, but most were quiet.

Not far from there they passed a small reconnaissance team already at work herding pigs out of an experimental trench. These were important pigs. They wore specially tailored uniforms that were made from a new synthetic fabric that the Army was testing, supposedly durable and lightweight, a promise for all future soldiers. The scientists had been disappointed when they failed to train the pigs to stand on their hind legs—more closely simulating humans—but the moment that Harry went off, the pigs were suddenly upright, standing, squealing, urinating, front hooves pawing the air. Dogs, monkeys, and burros were also somewhere out there being monitored in dry underground bunkers.

Closing in on ground zero—less than half a mile—the sparse landscape turned empty. Trucks and equipment that had been left there were gone, everything flash-burned into the minute particles that fell, ashlike, here and there as a strange rain. Five hundred yards out, the assault vehicles stopped, the rear ramps lowered, the soldiers disembarked and began to move in formation up the incline where the detonation tower, now vaporized, had stood. The ground everywhere was winter white, but hot. Above them, the desert dawn had been erased by heavy black clouds, smoke, floating debris.

Two hundred yards from center they stopped, and having fulfilled their orders and not knowing now exactly what to do, the sergeant stepped out front, smartly saluted ground zero, turned, and ordered the men to head back. With each heavy-booted step, the snowy dust and ash floated up so that from a distance the men looked as if they were moving, knee-deep, through clouds.

―――――――――

Elly and Lewis Barlow, our neighbors, were card players—experts at Hearts and No Knock Rummy, tender for a game that they taught my parents called Michigan. Winter nights the four of them would be hunched over a kitchen table, moaning about what they'd been dealt. My mother never held her cards in close enough and oftentimes my father got a peek at the queen of spades or at a run or he'd push her hand toward her chest and give her a warning. "Lorraine, you're showing us everything."

"Well, not everything," she'd say, putting her cards down and start-ing to unbutton her blouse. Lewis smacked his cards face down and clapped. Elly squealed and took the time to roll a cigarette—Prince Albert in a can. My father got up from the table, stood behind my mother, and wrapped his arms around her, as if that was the only way she could be stopped. "Okay, okay," he said, "I'm sorry."

Actually my parents were wrapped around each other like that almost half the time—embracing, clutching, hugging, pawing. With other men, my mother said she would have felt mauled, but with my father she felt her heart race, she felt her shoes suddenly wanting to be thrown off. They had sex like animals and she was not ashamed to say so: on a living room chair, in the root cellar, in the orchard during spring when the ribbon grass was still soft enough to make a bed. Nearby, I dozed or chewed my fist and waited.

My mother knew that leaving wouldn't be easy, and maybe that's another reason we headed for the Barlows that morning: comfort and an understanding shoulder. Elly and Lewis had lived a fairly bumpy life themselves—fast times and booze in Vegas casinos—and they looked on other people's trouble with gentle eyes.

My mother gauged that we had gone over two miles and were more than halfway there. We had passed the S curve in the road a while back and she thought we must be close to Carpenter Wash, but time and long brown vistas mingled and distorted both. She prodded the stroller to the side of the road, found a flat rock, and we sat facing each other.

"Huh, movies," she said. "What baloney. What trash."

Months before at a nearby filming site where my father was caring for the horses used in breakneck cavalry scenes, my mother had met a brawny blonde named Jeff Cantrell, an in-demand lead for B movies, and she was thoroughly unimpressed. Brusque and egotistical, he spent too much time dabbing perspiration from his face and yelling for someone to bring him iced tea, and when she learned that his real name was Ira Kaufmann, she was even more disgusted. "What, is he ashamed to use his real name?" she wanted to know. All the hubbub and shouting around the set didn't seem to foster any character in those people as far as she was concerned. Everyone was either whining or cussing or laughing with the fake high-pitched laughter that she identified as Hollywood.

Milo de Rossi hadn't shown her anything different. My father had escorted him around our ranch for several days, pointing out box canyons and high rocky fortresses, and by the second day de Rossi was convinced that this was the place for his movie, *Apache Sunset*. He already had Audie Murphy lined up, he said. He hoped for Anthony Quinn or Lee Marvin as the sad-eyed Apache leader who would glimpse the future and see the pain for which his people were bound. De Rossi was still new enough in the business to be regarded with hope, but his lack of financial foresight and his thudding story lines would finally catch up with him, and in the years ahead he was destined for junk.

Smoking fat Havana Cristo's, he took pleasure in confiding in everyone at dinner each night: William Holden had a drinking problem; sometimes had to be thrown in a shower before he could complete his scenes.

My mother shook her head as she served the venison or roast she had carefully prepared. Everyone ate as if they'd been deprived for months.

"Kirk Douglas?" he asked. "Know him? Gotta hire a full-time tutor to teach him his lines. Sorta like training a dog, I guess. A little thin between the old ears. Of course, this is only what I hear. I'm just passing it along."

My mother couldn't stand de Rossi's feral gaze when anything female moved past him. "Call me Milo, my dear," he had told her as she bent over the oven pulling out hot rolls.

"If I had the chance, I'd call him a lot worse than that," she told me as we sat at the side of the road. Her shoulder-length dark hair blew forward around her face, and with one hand she quickly gathered it up and held it at the back of her neck. With the other, she moved the stroller back and forth, gently rocking me in the sunshine. I babbled my heart out to her, kicked my feet, and squirmed in the cotton netting of the seat and these things she understood as my wanting to get back on the road. She picked up the suitcase, turned the stroller around, and shoved us forward.

By then, in the far-off distance ahead, the sky was changing and at first my mother wasn't concerned—a hundred changes rolled by each day in that enormous unpredictable sky—but as the disturbance came closer, she pushed more firmly against the stroller. From the first good look, she could see that it was not the deep pouting gray of a thunderhead. It was another one of those churning purple-black clouds from the test site, but it was larger this time and lower. In it, she saw sparks of light, glimmerings, electricity, she didn't know what.

"Nothing to worry about," she told me, though I wasn't worried. I was happy, totally entertained. The scenery slipped by, right and left, like wavy blue and brown streamers. I pointed randomly and screeched.

"Tree," she said. "Rock." "Fence." "Horse." "Mountain." She reeled off a vocabulary that I was at least a good six months away from, but she encouraged me to try anyway. She loved the sound of me, unlike Miss Lurl, my third-grade teacher who years later put tape over my mouth. "Miss Yakety Yak" she called me, and my schoolmates picked it up, chanted it at recess, whispered it down the rows at the spelling bee.

My mother and I passed Carpenter Wash and then the wind grew stronger and came in bursts. My mother's skirt clung to the front of her legs and flared out in back, waving behind her. She stopped, dug through the suitcase, took out a lacy white bonnet, and put it on me, drawing it down low over my forehead, tying the straps firmly beneath my soft clefted chins, which she couldn't resist pinching. My mother loved all of me, but it was my head that she had high hopes

57

for and therefore protected—a bonnet, a scarf, a ratty straw hat used for gardening. Sometimes, in the heat, she put a wet cloth on my head, water dripping down my neck and shoulders, my face scrunching up into a good cry, but she hushed me without any sympathy. She wanted me to be able to think, to reason, which is where the trouble lay for her.

My mother didn't have to reason that morning, however. A mother simply tastes trouble; she feels it in the small of her back or in her blood or somewhere along her jangly nerves. Even ten miles off and blowing toward her, trouble was about as discreet as an ocean liner full of singing drunks. My mother said she suddenly smelled something carried on the wind: lye and dust and burnt liver or kidney beans, an awful combination that made her gasp. She hadn't eaten much that morning and her stomach turned once and then she got ahold of herself. She dropped the suitcase right there in the road as if it was something that had become crude and pointless, and with both hands on the stroller she started running, barreling into the wind, pushing us madly up a small ridge from where, she hoped, we might be able to see the Barlows' windmill. The stroller wheels kept hitting rocks and ruts, but she powered through, sending the stroller sideways and the front end off the ground. I slid down in the seat, crumpled formless as a pillow, laughed and squealed and did my best to kick away my shoes.

On the broad Lincoln County range that runs from Nevada head-on into western Utah, sheep were grazing. The bells they wore jingled like a soft stuttering music out in no-man's land. These were western sheep, medium-sized and perseverant, muzzles down in sagebrush and galleta grass. Though spread out and foraging, they still moved as a loose ever-present herd.

The cloud blew over about nine that morning. The wind came with it, blowing to the east and then suddenly shifting north, stirring up dust devils, rolling tumbleweeds across the desert into the midst of the feeding sheep. They scattered with the noise and sudden movement. As the sky overhead turned dark, sheep dashed for cover that wasn't there. The bells on their necks clattered wildly, bringing more confusion and panic. A fine dusty mist began to fall from the cloud and, like rain, covered and penetrated: the dense layered wool of the sheep, the heavy-leafed sage. The sheep veered right and left, stumbled and doubled back on themselves, and even after the cloud had passed, the bleating continued. They hopped and skittered at a falling rock, at a shadow, at a waving branch. Finally they lowered their heads again, though the ground and plants were now covered with a film of ash which lent a strange new taste to sagebrush. Slowly they grazed their way into the next valley.

Not far away in Elgin, Nevada, three children came out of a trailer house and played in what they imagined to be snow. They spread their arms, ran in circles, and turned their faces up into the gray-white storm. The oldest one—the only one who could write—used her finger to trace her name through the snow collecting on the hood of a junked car in the driveway. She licked her finger to clean it and then cartwheeled while the two younger ones, in wet drooping diapers, made themselves dizzy spinning.

From there the cloud moved due east—Nevada into Utah, though there was no marked change from one place to the other. It was all just dry unrelenting terrain. Here and there, almost like accidents, a tarpapered house sprang up and next to it the rotted posts of an abandoned corral, and in those lonely places a Basque shepherd or a used-car salesman holding a Geiger counter looked up, wondered to himself, and shrugged.

A young husband, hauling furniture in his truck from Veyo to Santa Clara, was surprised by how the cloud seemed to engulf him and even to move with him down Highway 18. He'd driven in bad weather before, sometimes been able to outrun the big spring and summer cloudbursts if he caught them far enough on the horizon in time. Ten miles out of Veyo, though, this cloud had caught him, surrounding the truck in whirling sand. Particles hit the windshield and seeped through every crevice of the old Ford until even his clothes were covered with a fine light soot.

When he finally turned off the side road and moved onto Highway 91, which led into Santa Clara and then on into Las Vegas, he was surprised to find a roadblock set up next to the Texaco station. He shifted down, idled forward, then stopped his truck and got out. Hours later, before the young man was allowed to go, the deputies burned his clothes, patted his shoulder to reassure him, and let him borrow a Texaco uniform to wear home. Even with her own furniture in the back of the truck, his wife didn't know him when he drove up to their house and stepped out of the cab.

My mother's lungs burned from running. Her arms and shoulders felt disconnected and one of her ankles was swelling, and by then she realized the stroller wasn't worth the trouble. She picked me up out of it, wrapped me in her arms, and she wished, for once, that there was more of her to cradle and cover me. She had run herself out, so she trotted on from there, off balance and heavy-footed, alternately watching the sky and the road and me.

Coming in fast from the southwest, the cloud grew larger, its edges spreading like thin fingers. In the midmorning sky it appeared to be a piece of boiling twilight that had broken away from somewhere else. Instinctively my mother moved over to the far side of the road, putting a little more distance between it and us.

I worked my arm away from my mother's chest and touched her

chin and talked to her in code—coos and broken syllables and among them she was almost positive that she heard the name John. Had the moment been different, she would have stopped, sat me in her lap, and we would have had a heart-to-heart, but as it was, we kept going.

My mother had shaken John Wayne's hand and that was about all. He was making arrangements for his upcoming movie, *The Conqueror,* in which he would play Genghis Khan and tempt Susan Hayward with his made-up almond eyes. It would be filmed not far from our ranch and he wanted to look things over, make some plans for his sons who would accompany him. Someone had given him a cup of coffee. My mother remembered Wayne stirring in two teaspoons of sugar and drinking the coffee so slowly that it had to be ice cold when he got to the bottom. He nodded his head shyly when they were introduced, stood up out of his chair and extended his hand, and she could see that he was a big sensitive meatblock of a man.

Sometimes in panic and in trying to protect our life, my mother forgot things about the movies: the sweet temperate nature of John Wayne, the way Milo de Rossi had written my father a large check for his and my mother's hospitality and it was that very check that gave us Christmas that year. My mother unwrapped her dream of a sewing machine and cried on and off all day.

A mother's intuition is seldom wrong and my mother's was always right about her babies. If she was mostly right about Milo de Rossi, she was absolutely right about that cloud. We had to find shelter.

She had taken only two steps off the road—toward a feeble overhang in the rocks—when she heard the long frantic blasts of a horn. My father, like a man driven by deep stinging forces that we couldn't understand, had ingeniously spliced the ignition on the old Dodge flatbed and gunned his way to find us. His puzzlement and fear had grown by leaps as he found first the suitcase in the road and then the abandoned stroller.

At the sound of the horn my mother turned and scanned the road behind until finally she could see the grill and the familiar green hood and the brown trail of road dust. She put her arm in the air and waved.

When finally he was next to us, my father opened his door, the engine still running, and came around and opened the other door for us. They didn't say a word, didn't give each other the cool slender glance of people still carrying grudges. With me held closer than ever to her chest, my mother skip-hopped onto the running board and then up onto the seat, looked straight ahead, and waited for my father to slam the door.

My father, of course, thought she was coming back for him. He couldn't stand two hours without her and he thought she felt the same, and in a while she did. But at the moment when she had jumped into the truck, she was all mother, all pounding heart, and she didn't for one second analyze our escape.

We drove back to the house while behind us, in the valley to the west, in the very spot where *The Conqueror* would be filmed the next year, the cloud unloaded sheer white dust and here and there glassy particles that would end up driving the cameramen wild, sudden glints and glarings appearing in the uncut footage. Sitting in the truck that day, we didn't know it, but my father would be there at that filming, too, maybe not a star but at least an extra. For weeks, dressed in blousy pants and wearing snow boots, he was destined to ride a skittish buckskin a hundred times across the same stretch of red sand until someone finally yelled that they had a take.

My father, glad to have his wife and daughter back that day, drove carefully and watched in his rearview mirror; my mother kept turning around. They didn't know exactly what they were seeing back there, but they were spooked, and in no time she had slid across the seat and partnered back up with him. The cloud hung low for a while and didn't seem to move. Beneath it, wind and dust and fallout created a turbulent hothouse that we could see and would hear about on the radio the next day.

Maybe to calm herself, my mother started—right there in the truck—by kissing my father's cheek, even though it was a little too smooth for her taste, a little too much like a young James Stewart's. Then things fell into place: a kiss, a hug, my mother's skirt coming up over her legs.

As my father was trying to drive with one hand, trying to sneak quick views of the road ahead, I told him, in the only way that I could—with grunts and aaahs and jibberish—that I loved him, whatever he was going to be.

In the months and years that followed after we safely arrived home, Telsa was exploded, Priscilla, Diablo, and Hood. There were others we didn't learn the names of. They drifted overhead, engraving a darkness in the sky, but they only appeared to pass and move into the shimmering distance.

Nature's Way

Close to midnight, they finally broke the lock and convinced her to get out of the bathtub, that she needed to see a doctor. She was Navajo and had been sitting in the steaming water for hours. She'd miscarried and all that stuff was floating in the water, too. After that, nobody in the dorm would use the bathtub. It was like voodoo or filth, something that could be picked up, or simply something that reminded us how death bloomed from our own clear bodies, too.

They lifted her up gently, but even so, I could tell it hurt. Her face was pinched in pain or weariness. She was smooth and heavy, and her wet hair stuck lifelessly to her back. Someone had brought a robe for her. It was winter and the cold of the dorm penetrated with a needle-like precision. You wouldn't believe how white a Navajo can turn, standing in that cold, bleeding.

They led her down the hallway, and I guess to Gloria's car, then on to the hospital. I really didn't know this girl, but when she stepped from the tub she did a curious thing that has made me think of her again and again. She closed her eyes, deliberately closed her eyes. She kept them closed down the hallway and perhaps even in Gloria's '72 Valiant as it reduced Flagstaff Highway to nothing but a cold, black line. I don't know why she closed her eyes and kept them closed, Gloria urging her to take step after step. It was like the blind leading the blind: the Navajo girl who had just miscarried and Gloria, our dorm manager, lonely and confused.

"This is what happens when you're fifty, sweeties," and Gloria would pull the elastic belt on her robe and let it snap back. We were never quite sure what this demonstration was supposed to divulge, but she would follow it up by pointing at her face and remarking on the disgusting enlargement of her pores. "Don't let anyone kid you," she'd tell us. "Life only gets uglier, meaner." She lived at the far end of the hall in a special apartment. She had a patchwork rug she had made herself, and a small TV with large rabbit ears. She continually complained about the reception, and raised hell if the stairwells weren't kept clean. Though she often mixed up our names and got the dates for our fire drills confused, Gloria did well that night, letting the Navajo girl lean against her in the darkness cut only by stars and pine tops.

I don't know why I have to see these things: the Navajo in the bathtub, the miserable way we reconcile ourselves to our lives. I was going to take a shower. I had shaved my legs and washed my hair. I could hear them beating on the door nearby, calling for her to come out. The water on my back was hot and furious, yet the commotion called me, too. When they broke the lock and opened the door, the milky steam rolled out upon the cold hall air.

Sometimes it takes years to fully see things. I think back upon this scene and see the small things: the soap, the toenails painted red, Gloria's hands as they attempted to comfort.

We went back to our rooms and talked about it, how they have to stop the bleeding, sometimes with drugs, sometimes surgically. "It's nature's way," Dawn Kramer added, though we all ignored her, for what this prima donna from Chicago knew about nature wouldn't have filled a single page. For weeks after, I thought about the Navajo girl and the way she closed her eyes, what she was shutting in or shutting out.

Like I said, none of us ever used that bathtub again, which was an unfortunate thing, for baths are healthy and soothing. They enfold us, they bring light to the mind, and they emulate the water from which life so warily crept millions of years ago.

Gloria returned in her Valiant the next morning, hushing us, telling us to mind our own business. The Navajo girl, she finally said, was fine, though she left school permanently for her home in Window Rock. I've never been there, but I like that name. I like the idea of a window in a rock—an opening in a black, hard space—a sliver's passage into the soul.

Dixon

First, it is not true that my brother Dixon went crazy in Vietnam—chewed his fingernails completely off and gutted a Huey helicopter in a rage when his R and R was suddenly bagged. Hell, Dixon never was in Vietnam. His three years in the Air Force were mostly spent in Biloxi where he was assigned to the motor pool and stayed long weekends in Gulfport on windy beaches with sand in his eyes and his shoulders constantly sunburned. He's buried now in a small cemetery called Dutchman's Acre, a place so quiet and green that it doesn't rightfully belong to this earth. Yeah, sure, he was big enough to gut a helicopter, but Dixon was slow and calm, and he always respected what wasn't his.

That's why the story about Dixon and Misty Waters doesn't make any sense either, because Misty was somebody else's wife, and Dixon may have liked to tease her—he might have even thought she was pretty—but as he used to say to me, his oldest sister, "It's clear as day on the insurance form. She's somebody else's beneficiary."

I'll tell you—crudeness does not know when to stop. There are versions of the Dixon-Misty story that put those two in the Texaco and Mobil gas station rest rooms going at it, full tilt, right up on those dirty counters next to where the rusted sinks are always dripping. Never any toilet paper or hand towels in those places. The mirrors cracked and filthy. Mind you—all of this on Misty's half-hour lunches from the bank. If Dixon were alive, he'd die at the thought of himself banging away to the tune of impact wrenches, some big Buick getting its tires rotated nearby.

But it was the dead twin story that brought my mother to her breaking point. She marched into my kitchen one morning not so long ago, and she said that my father was too old, so it was up to me to stop all this horse trash about Dixon. Her hands were shaking and there were big tears in her eyes. My mother is barely five feet tall, Dixon's death has been a real setback for her, and standing there dressed in one of her bright golf outfits—though she's never played a day of golf in her life—she presented a petite but imposing argument.

"Mom," I told her, sitting at the table, still in my robe, "I love to see you, but I wish you'd call before you drop in." I was eating a bowl of Cheerios and, like a kid, reading the back of the box, trying to get my energy up. Mornings are hard on me. The good, deep sleep I used to have has become a rare commodity; I toss and turn, drift in and out of a dark fitfulness. I think rather than dream.

"What? You think your seventy-year-old father should go defend Dixon's name? Wake up, Hillary," she said, her hands on her boxy hips, a pose she assumes for the most serious subjects that intrude on her life. "Being part of a family isn't a free ride, you know. There's responsibility and it's looking you square in the face. I'll admit that Dixon had his hard times and did not always think in a straight line, but what I'm hearing about him is absurd and downright mean. Wherever he is," she said, looking awkwardly up and then left and right, "he doesn't deserve this."

For the most part, my family believes in good citizenship, not religion, so it was difficult when Dixon died. We had no place to send him—no beautiful, light-filled landscape to imagine him in. Yet, even without a heaven, we found ourselves still thinking of Dixon as being somewhere, though when we spoke of him we never knew in which direction to refer. We craned our heads upward, or, then embarrassed, we peered far out beyond the freeway to the muted horizon.

I have never liked being trapped in a corner where suddenly all the alternatives are savagely reduced, but that's just where my mom had me. I turned forty-one last December and that's old enough to talk and think for yourself, though age has no meaning when your mother tells you she's hit rock bottom and needs your help. Dixon was her only son, her first and probably last mystery, the one she made cherry pie for, the one who would send her to a chair laughing at his knock-knock jokes or his imitations of the latest dances. Once, demonstrating the moon walk for us, he backed right off the front porch and corkscrewed his elbow hard into the ground. Had to wear a sling for two weeks, and if you asked him about it, Dixon just laughed and said he'd do anything to get a two-week prescription of codeine.

Everything else you've heard about Dixon, all the little pieces of gossip that have floated your way, they hold about as much truth as a wet sock. I know that most nights Gordon Jenner can be found in a local bar yakking away about somebody, and more often than not, it's Dixon. Jenner puts his feet up on the table, and he tries to make a living off my brother—stories of Dixon in camouflage and war paint, of Dixon wrecking cars and just walking away from them, the smoke spiraling up and the gas tanks about to blow. But Jenner has silt for brains. He's lived too long down in Hillam raising those blue-ribbon Charolais and married to a woman who, after ten years in this country, still speaks only Japanese. Oh, I'm not saying it isn't pretty to hear her bent over the flowers in their garden, sing-songing her language under a blue sky, but what the hell is she saying? She could be complimenting your clothes or telling you to go diddle yourself, and you'd stand there, just like I have plenty of times, with a big dumb well-digger's grin plastered on your face.

Jenner has always played stupid, said he doesn't know what I'm talking about. "Look," I told him, my hands deep in my pockets, "I'm not accusing anybody, but there are some crazy things being said about Dixon, and I just want them to stop."

He stood there leaning against his truck, his arms folded across his barrel chest, his tanned face like an old sunbaked apple. "Now what interest would I have in talking about the dead?" he asked me. I didn't have an answer for that because I truthfully don't know what's in Jenner's head, though with a man like him a hatchet and a pair of tweezers would be the easiest way to find out.

Jenner is pigeon-hearted and about a million miles away from knowing Dixon. Even when my brother pinned his last dollar bill to the inside of his flannel shirt and started walking toward Santa Fe, he had fire and smarts, he had years of good looks left in him, and the dashing honesty of a real live prince.

———————

The dead twin story spread in waves through our small Kentucky town, first through the graineries and discount hardware outlets, then through beauty salons and dime stores, and finally settled in the worn linoleumed kitchens that are the heart of this community. It was a lackluster little tale which basically seized on the opportunity to make a monster of the baby Dixon.

"Rolled over and suffocated his own little twin for an extra god-damned bottle of milk. The newspaper sort of covered it up. April 14, 1949, you mark me. They called it a baby sudden death. Huh!" Jenner's stories started going that far back, reaching crazily into the black side of his make-believe.

Lloyd Ebson's kid was tending bar that night at Crazy Eights and he told me just how Jenner leaned back in his chair when the talk lulled, and told that little story, and when his listeners were appropriately quiet and stung, he called over to Ebson's kid to order him up a fried egg sandwich, then dowsed it with ketchup and mustard and Tabasco when it came. It made Ebson's kid half-sick to see fresh eggs treated that way.

Somewhere between Canasta and her volunteer days at the public library, my mother heard all about Dixon and his twin, and, like I said, it hit her hard as concrete. That's when she came asking for my help with those big tears in her eyes, her voice high-pitched and breathy—just on the edge of those old-woman sobs that can wrench your gut and turn your will to toothpaste.

"Hey," I told her that day as she stood uninvited in my kitchen, "I've talked to Jenner and he just denies everything. What do you want me to do? Get an attorney?"

"You're a smart girl," she said. "You run a business and manage to take a couple of vacations a year. I know you'll figure something out."

But it was not that easy. I spent days staking out plans to stop Jenner, then gave them up when they became ridiculous even to me. I wrote three different letters to him, each one becoming surlier, each one falling further away from intelligible correspondence. I didn't send any of them. Late at night, my patience and creativity mostly used up, I slipped into visions of tire slashing and low-grade arson— you know, garbage cans or at most a toolshed. I tried to envision myself holding a gun—small caliber—something sharp and clean and plenty intimidating, but I remembered what my father had told me: "Unless you're willing to fire it, a piece of metal is not very persuasive."

I have always settled the conflicts in my life with the easiest, most accommodating methods I know of—whatever that says about me. When Armand, my ex-husband, and I parted company, he wanted to take the new Ethan Allen living room set with him to Atlanta and I wanted it to stay, so I took a quarter from my purse, flipped it, and told him to call. He paid two neighborhood boys to help him load it into the U-Haul, although Armand was an exercise nut, and as it turned out, he was able to lift the sectional into the van himself. He wore an old pair of cutoffs that day, and when I saw him bend over and haul up that furniture, his legs hard and muscled as a ropewalker's, everything in me wanted him to stay, and if it hadn't been for my pride, which disguises itself as indigestion, I would have walked out there, kissed him, and asked him to extend my credit. He drove off that night, even though the second gear of the U-Haul was whining like a sick cat, and then two years later Dixon was dead and it seemed to me that my losses were mounting in a reckless way.

I don't know how to measure the empty place that those two left in me—meteor crater or the bottomless, black sinkhole my father scared us with when we were kids at bedtime. If it's true that Armand stole my heart, then Dixon took some other vital organ, because I swear, the world around me just does not feel the same. Nothing smells as good as it once did: the sweet hickory of a summer barbecue, the soap on a man's skin that used to haunt me for days. It's all gone, vanished. Just a puff of black smoke, and then the piercing white light of an empty room.

The word *karate* would have never interested me. It was the telephone number 588-KICK that kept running through my head. I heard it on the radio about fifty times a day—a major ad campaign, I guess, and it worked. When I called, I expected an Oriental voice to answer—a Shing Lu or a Chan Chung—but it was Tony Ramirez—owner, master, fifth-degree black belt—who said, "Tuesday is when you begin."

Certainly I was naive. Definitely I was grasping at straws. I did not have the total scheme laid out in my mind, but I knew that I needed to equip myself in some way to bring Gordon Jenner to the silence that seemed ripe and waiting for him.

And then, too, the stakes had been upped when my mother made a scene in a local Safeway. She spotted Jenner's wife on the produce aisle, and when Mom could get no response from her as to what her husband had against Dixon, she started chasing the other woman through the store, imploring her to tell what she knew. There they were, each pushing those big unwieldy carts, running up and down the aisles until my mother banked her cart into a canned goods display and had her forehead engraved with a 16-ounce can of green beans.

Tony Ramirez, my karate instructor, would have given Mom this advice: "The goal is not to look where you're going, but to see." In the first weeks of class I had no idea what he meant by that, and he never gave any explanations, just told me to repeat the basic forms again and again. I'd stand over at the side of the bare classroom and complete twenty high blocks, then twenty low ones, and then I'd combine them. If I was lucky, he would nod his head at me and tell me to give it another round. There was no sport or art to Ramirez's way of thinking; it was all discipline. Once he made me stand in a corner of the classroom and practice my karate shout, the *kiai*. "Listen to yourself," he said. "Get used to that sound." At first I was somewhat embarrassed to stand in the corner and yell at myself—the "uts" and "huhs" supposedly coming up from the diaphragm—but finally some layer of self-consciousness fell away and the shouting felt good, invigorating.

Dixon was never embarrassed by anything that I knew of, though maybe he should have been. Standing up in front of the church as best man at his friend's wedding, Dixon—after too much preceremony champagne—let out a horrendous belch, and then he just looked up at the ceiling, like maybe the rafters were slightly shifting or a thunderstorm was threatening the day.

My brother did not, I repeat, did not moon the bride's mother later during the reception, and whatever charges were filed for indecent exposure at that celebration had nothing to do with Dixon. All I will say about that incident was that the bride's mother was a

Joan Crawford look-alike who presided like an old witch over the hot hors d'oeuvre table, but quite honestly Dixon was passed out in the coat room by then, peaceful with a couple of big synthetic fur coats wrapped around him.

I would have been a lot more comfortable at Dixon's funeral if someone had laid a couple of those fur coats around him in his coffin, made him look like he was just sleeping through another party. I think everybody we ever knew was at that funeral. Misty Waters was there, poured into a little black dress no bigger than a glove. If she would have had to bend over for anything, I guarantee that no seam in that dress could have possibly survived. Dixon would have enjoyed that kind of spectacle—a flash of surprise and then a lot of bare skin. I asked him once if Misty Waters was her real name, and he said he didn't know, but he thought it fit her perfectly. Names didn't mean much to him.

They didn't mean much to Tony Ramirez either, who walked slowly around the classroom and observed his students with a cold trigger eye. He addressed all individuals as "you," and though it sounds as if he was distant and intimidating, that impression of him instantly vanished when he demonstrated his tournament style. Ramirez moved with nothing but pure love of each moment: the cat stance, the shoulder grab, a rousing roundhouse kick. Ramirez didn't fight; he stalked. His balance and speed were hypnotic. He could kick and pivot like a dancer, the only difference being that his kick could and would break your ribs. When he showed us his Heaven and Earth, a series of blocks and punches punctuated by shouts, I knew that I had come to the right place. I could see then that what Gordon Jenner needed more than anything else was to feel Heaven and Earth descending on him.

~~~~~~~~~~

The one I heard the other night—it came to me in pieces, a little from Pete Myers and some from Dorothy Carter—is how Dixon crawled all the way from Pioneer Park down to Preston High School, baying like a moon-crazed dog and slobbering all down his shirt, dark frothy spit that looked like he'd been eating dirt. That's a real Jenner touch—the dirt—something to get you gagging.

You use your head, though—step off the distance from the park to the high school and see if it isn't damn near impossible to do on your hands and knees. All that gravel and rotten pavement. Dixon would have been hamburger. Supposedly Jenner saw him on the side of the road, stopped and tried to get him into the car, but Dixon's eyes were glazed over, he stunk like catfish bait, and he was not to be reasoned with.

Funny how the truth gets twisted, because the fact is, Dixon was a supremely reasonable man. He thought things out. He would look at a broken vacuum cleaner and step by step he would take it apart, clean it up, and make it work again, the suction so strong you'd best not get it near your feet. When Hawk Lewis was determined to cut down a hundred-year-old oak on his side property and all the neighbors had given up convincing him otherwise, it was Dixon who walked down to his house one night with a couple of root beers and somehow got him to fall in love with that tree again. It was a huge, beautiful oak loaded with magpies and starlings, and the one thing Dixon said he told Hawk was that trees could indeed feel pain, and how would Hawk like a chain saw in his side?

The crazy thing is, Dixon did have a twin, an unnamed baby boy who never even went home from the hospital. In fact, he was never named because he lived less than two hours. "He just wasn't ready to breathe" is what my mother told us.

Someone has to be pretty bored to take that little sadness from so long ago, mix it up, and throw in a baby killer like Gordon Jenner has done. A smart guy would have chosen somebody else to tell that story about, because if you traced Dixon back to a kid you'd see someone with the little teaspoon face of an angel, and you'd know that Dixon's instincts and nature were as clear and harmless as water from his very start.

I'm not saying he was perfect, but right down to his bones Dixon was good. Once, as kids, I tried to get him to steal candy with me, and as soon as I'd told him the plan, his hands were paralyzed—he said he felt ice all through his fingers. Years later, when Francine Johnson put the moves on him one night, he just didn't have the heart to tell her to go bark at someone else. All the bad genes of three generations of Johnsons had settled in Francine—in her face, to be exact. Dixon took her home that night, which amazed me because he had an epic appeal to women—he could be wearing a baseball cap and dirty levis and in ten minutes he'd have some exotic female rooted deep as a mulberry right next to him. "So why Francine Johnson?" I asked him.

He shrugged and put his feet up on the dashboard of my car. "In the dark," he said, "with the lights off, everything evens out."

~~~~~~~~

Some people don't know when to shut up. "Diarrhea of the mouth," my mother calls it, but I think it can signal something much worse— a bitter heart no bigger or better than a turnip.

What Jenner has to be bitter about, I don't know. There are no easy windows by which to look into another person's life, so I judge it from the outside—what he does and says, if he has a dog and feeds it, how he treats his mate.

I was good to my ex-husband, but good doesn't necessarily mean close or bonded, it doesn't mean you sleep cradled like two spoons at night, or that your future can stretch scary as hell like a suspension bridge out in front of you and as long as the two of you are together it doesn't matter. Although he never settled to just one woman, Dixon knew all about couples and he warned me about Armand. "Love him or lose him," he said, and he was right.

If I had a dollar for every time Dixon was right . . . well. The one time he was wrong, though, he was seriously wrong. That was when he took off for Santa Fe, thinking his life here had stalled. He could walk it, he said—hell, cancer patients and paraplegics were crisscrossing the continent and he could do it, too. Adventure and bullheadedness always flowed together in Dixon like one muddy river. The fact that he started out on that trip with only a few dollars didn't scare him. Dixon believed you could build your life up out of nothing—just like a fence—a brick at a time.

On an Oklahoma two-way road in the oil-colored twilight is where it ended for my brother when a semi came up over a rise and could not distinguish Dixon from the shadows. His hair was dark. He wore an old brown corduroy jacket that became even browner after he rolled more than fifty feet in the dirt. I went down there to *identify* him, which after an accident like that is just a loose term, because the person I saw only vaguely resembled my brother.

Dixon robbed the bank when he got his looks. He was big and lean, had a square jaw and a natural kind of abandoned grace when he moved. I'll admit that I got the deep-water eyes in the family, but Dixon got the hair—thick and wavy, the kind you want to run your hand through for good luck. More than once, he was mistaken for the Olympic swimmer Mark Spitz, and sometimes, good-naturedly, he'd play along and say that going for the gold isn't all it's cracked up to be.

It was only natural that people at his funeral were shocked when they saw Dixon. For a while I heard the stuff about the whole top of his head having to be sewn back on, but the worst was about his ears—plastic imitations that would surely outlast the rest of him. I know how it went on from there—how he was flying on LSD and ran straight toward the lights of that truck—you know, the old moth to the flame. How my mother tried to climb into the coffin with her only son when she first walked into the memorial service. How the big heart-shaped arrangement of tulips was secretly from the fire chief's wife. The problem is, if you were mining any of that for the truth, you'd be digging all the way to China.

~~~~~~~~~~

Tony Ramirez told us one day that it is an endless path, this karate. I didn't have forever, though, so I asked him if I could double up on classes—take two a week. He shrugged and said, "Take three a week, but it may not happen any faster."

I had been his student for several months, and I knew his whole lecture about the most formidable opponent being ourselves, but that did not change what happened in Kentucky Fried Chicken last Friday night. I was waiting for a 15-piece bucket when Jenner walked in— a pair of dusty Dingo boots and a big moth-eaten suede hat—that's how I saw him. He didn't acknowledge me in any way, just kept looking at the menu board as if this was the biggest decision of his life. I hated that he wouldn't look at me.

People don't get to choose when things happen, and if you ask me, real talent is taking events as they occur and making them count. Luck would have had me running into Jenner in a couple of months, but happenstance put the two of us right there that night with a big black and red picture of the Colonel smiling down at us. The counter girl delivered my bucket of chicken, and as I turned to head toward the door I said "hey" to Jenner. He looked down, kind of startled, and what I did next surprised even me. I walked over to the straw dispenser, not much more than a wooden box, and I gave it an edge-of-hand strike and the box splintered and a few straws rolled down onto the floor. Just a few plastic straws, but God, they were beautiful to me. I stared over at Jenner, didn't say a word, actually couldn't. I was gritting my teeth against the white hot pain in my hand, but he didn't know that. All he knew—and I could tell this from his big fool blue eyes—was that Heaven and Earth were on their way.

Tony Ramirez looked at my hand and this week he's making me practice with the twelve- and thirteen-year-old beginners, but I don't care. There is a certain satisfaction I get in towering over all of my classmates. And my karate shout is the strongest one in this class.

I'm not like some of the people in this town who have grown radar ears, but I do hear things. Eleanor Goodway, one of my mother's oldest friends, came into my insurance office the other day. I was surprised because she has both term and whole life policies up to her ears, but she was there for a different reason. "Hillary," she said, bending over my desk, lowering her voice as if this was privileged information, "chicken is nothing to lose your head over. I know these fast food places gyp you every once in a while—more legs than breasts, or the biscuits are a day old—but to break a plate-glass window over ten dollars worth of food . . ." She shook her head at me the way she's been shaking her head at this whole town for the last fifty years. She took a handkerchief out and dabbed at her nose and the smell of her lilac water drifted through the State Farm office. I didn't have to ask her who she had been talking to.

Jenner is one thing; he's in the category of fleas and ticks. Dixon is another. If he had been in Vietnam, as the story goes, I'm sure he would have been a hero. He would have somehow saved a child or woman in that junkyard jungle or at a point when everything was blown bare he would have stooped down and cradled a man's cantalouped head in a dying moment.

Dixon left me with all these what-if's, and for the most part, I'll warn you, brothers are like that. They'll live and laugh and make it so dreams won't come near your house, won't even park on your street.

Simple Yellow Cloth

~~~~~~

My eyes open and quickly the water of my sleep clears. It's Thursday night. At first I'm angry because it's past one and I have to go to work the next day. Daria is out there in the hallway and she's humming something that I can't name, and maybe it's because I've just been awakened suddenly, but the vague familiarity of that song is driving me crazy. There's a formula for remembering things; it's like walking backwards. It's based on the premise that every movement and thought is connected, and that by being methodical we can find anything: our shoes, our keys, our very lives. At night, however, I am not prone to reason or formula, though if there were an easy way to get my daughter back into bed right now, I'd use it.

"Daria," I call, and I know she hears me but she doesn't answer, which is a kind of formula itself: a tiny fist that opens with nothing in it. I move to the other side of the bed and sit up. From there, I can see her sitting by the night light, her legs crossed, her arms folded, a winter child who is completely of my own making. Not that I brag about it. It's something I usually keep to myself. And mind you, it has no religious significance. Daria is a child created purely from my own desire, the repetition of my dreams, and the leftover Christmas candles I burned every night. Not magic, but will.

Don't misunderstand. I like men. I like how they puff their cheeks out when they shave, and how they walk, and how they are really unable to lie effectively. In a given room on a given night I can turn and be totally undone by the sight of a man as he reaches for a drink. For me, the line that his arm makes as he reaches out is the very line between all passion and restraint. I've been in love twice and either of those men could have been Daria's father, but neither is.

"Daria," I call again, and this time she looks up, and I swear, being childless was a curse. The first time I held her, there was a stone thrown into a pool and I knelt in the cattail and reeds, alive, attentive. Between us, a life exists on its own, something with heart and claws, a thing still kneeling at the pool. "Please go back to bed," I tell her, at which point she increases the volume of her song and turns away from me. That's what she's like. That's how calm and undisturbed she is in the middle of the night. It makes me flinch a little, for my daughter in the hallway has a voice that unfolds like paper, words that make sense only because she says them with such confidence. I'm sleepy and yet I marvel at her.

Don't think this has all been a joy, though. My pregnancy was long and troublesome, which I attribute to the fact that Daria's conception was a bit out of the ordinary. For over two months I worked at it. The concentration it took was intense and I started losing weight. My mother would come by and ask what was up, I looked so pale, was that jerk David bothering me again?

I had to think of objects repeatedly, things that have meaning: Chopin's back at the piano as the rain slowly destroyed the midsummer holiday. The glow-in-the-dark stars I pasted on my ceiling above the bed like a piece of the night sky Lo Fen-Lang had bought for a concubine before his dynasty crumbled. At my bedside, the Christmas candles burned hot and true. By the twelfth of May I knew I was pregnant.

I'm determined to wait her out tonight. "Children learn by watching you," my mother has explained. "Be calm and let her see what you want her to do."

Daria knows I don't allow her to sleep with me, so she's been making her way to the hall in the middle of the night where she sings and plays until she gets sleepy again. She always wakes me up when she's out there, and sometimes I feel guilty letting her fall asleep on the floor, but I think the alternatives are worse.

I tell her good night and lie back down, but if I move my feet to the side I can still see her: yellow nightgown, hair loose and wild from the braid she wore today.

Sitting there in the hallway, Daria is the promise that the world will be all right. When she plays store, she uses Milk Duds for money. I hear her counting "eight, twenty, one hundred" to her customers. I tell her to stay off the sofa, chocolate makes a mess, and she listens to me. Already there is such possibility in our lives.

That Daria has no father is a fact that should engage us in an interesting conversation some day. I'll simply tell her what I know: that any law can be bent, that what is certainly freakish to some has been a moment of confounding beauty to another. I'll cook something like a salmon and have it open on the table, red and inviting, with cut lemon and mint.

And slowly Daria's song wavers. For a minute I almost think I can make out "The Twelve Days of Christmas," but then I realize she couldn't possibly know all of that song with its web of verses. Daria stretches out and becomes simple yellow cloth or the yellow birds on my grandmother's clothesline in the fall when the afternoon sun subdues everything in its warmth. When I'm sure she's asleep, I carry her into her own bed.

I check the time when I come back to my room. It's almost two. Sometimes I get too worried about sleep, how I'll feel the next day. Some people do fine on four or five hours, but I need seven or eight if I'm going to think. I start to get into bed, then stand back up and pull my nightshirt off. I walk around to the right side of the bed, the side that usually stays perfectly made, and I draw the covers back and get in. I look up at Lo Fen-Lang's stars that in the desert sky must seem like cut foil or nickel, a blister's flame. When I close my eyes, there is only darkness, which, in itself, is a concert of sleep and dreams. This time I'm working on a boy.

Wintercourse

~~~~~~

Lorna came to us in the first big snow at the end of November, flushed up as strays often are in the sudden cold. Dogs, cats—anything old, nearsighted, or temporarily lame. They look for a garage or a warm light or even a fleece-lined boot that's been left out overnight. Under our back deck near the steamy underside of our hot tub, Bruce and I found a small, sickly bear eating scavenged pizza from a half-crushed box early one morning, the peppery smell of sausage drifting up from beneath the wood planks. In no time, Fish and Game was here—eight men in heavy coats trying to decide what to do, while the bear simply rolled over, stretched out like an old shaggy rug, and fell into the depths of a garlicky sleep.

Like most of those storms, the big one that November began as ordinary gray sky settling in just above the treetops and then letting loose with the clean, white powder that this stretch of Colorado is known for—Hermosa north to Silverton, with Purgatory looming between, a place we try to stay away from. Everything outside was silent, frozen—postcard pretty but raw and staggering when the wind came up.

The snow, already up to the windowsills, had finally slowed when Lorna rang our doorbell and stood out there trembling, the Sysco truck and grinning driver she had hitched a ride with creeping backward down our long drive. Slouched and unperturbed, she looked like someone who intimately knows the in's and out's of bus depots everywhere. There were dark circles around her eyes: either two-day-old mascara or late nights and tension. In one of the packs she carried—though we didn't find this out for a while—was a midnight special, so cold and gray and unreal looking that when I finally saw it I thought it was a toy or one of those crazy cigarette lighters. Her hair had been cut close to the scalp, and from the looks of her bony figure she had almost used herself up in El Paso. Before that, it had been Atlanta, and before that, an unsuccessful stay at the University of Florida where two security guards had removed her bodily from a chemistry lab.

At first when Bruce, her father, saw her standing on our doorstep— a thin, smiling savage with the snow lightly whirling around her— he went momentarily blank. "All of a sudden she was standing there looking like she'd been living on the streets and I couldn't get my breath, Eileen," he told me later, running his hand through his hair, which is what he does when things just don't add up or make him nervous.

Unfortunately I missed that moment—the long-lost daughter greeting her weak-kneed dad. Actually I was upstairs on a ladder painting mine and Bruce's bedroom a soft erotic blue—two shades lighter than the color of water. I had the salesman at the paint store mix it special for me. The woman behind me in the checkout line—a Broncos cap and a very thin cigarette is what I remember of her—asked what

I was painting, and when I told her my bedroom and she saw the sample color on the lid, she understood. She winked at me and blew on her fingernails. "Whoa. Watch out," she told me, and we smiled, not knowing each other, but knowing the same things about how the world works, what colors lead to love and beyond.

I had left the store happy that day with two gallons of flat acrylic, navigating the ice and slush and cars of the busy parking lot. To my left, the passenger door of a station wagon tolerated the weight of a woman's dangling body, her feet flying back and forth, crablike, as she tried to find a foothold on the glazed asphalt. The knife-edged north wind had caught the hem of her long skirt and ballooned it into a colorful awning, revealing, beneath, a chewed-up black slip and mismatched socks. A heavy man scurried from the other side of the car to help her. He bent and offered her his arm and the thick ham of his shoulder. "Come on," he yelled, "get up," while she scrambled and groaned. I held my breath for her.

Frustration runs high in this weather. Our friend Noah Raye, for instance, found a tire iron in his hands and his windshield splintered into oblivion. He did the job himself when his Jeep stalled and left him stranded down on Highway 160 while Jim Littlefoot's bachelor party went right on without him—two kegs, a cake, and the dancing Ramos twins.

In the midst of November and cold and all this tension, however, I found the smell of paint calming—deep and ethery, the smell of sex chemicalized. I opened our bedroom windows and cranked up the heat. I threw an old blanket over the bedroom floor as a drop cloth, and I already had one wall painted—cool blue and misty, as if there was no wall there, but only our bed and dresser and then the sky veering upward—and I had started on the ceiling when I heard Bruce calling me from downstairs. I had a bandana tied over my hair and a swipe of blue paint under my nostrils. I was wearing the mechanic's jump suit that Bruce uses when he works on the truck—

actually fiddles with it and cusses and then throws his hands up and finally takes it to the Chevron station. I waited, and when he called me again I plodded down the stairs, holding the paint roller like a flag and wanting to know what was so damn important.

Lorna was standing there; I guess you could say my stepdaughter, since I am Bruce's wife now and my life seems to be quickly moving outward from me like rings of water: woman, wife, stepmother. I'd never met Lorna before; Bruce hadn't seen her in over two years. We stood in the entryway and offered simple introductions, and in minutes it felt as if we had used up all the air and were teetering on the dangerous edge of nothing left to say. Bruce coughed, thank God, and took several steps back and invited Lorna into the living room, where she began to unlayer herself.

She took off a large black denim jacket, an aged wool muffler, and two khaki military sweaters, and beneath all the Army-Navy Surplus attire Lorna turned out to be pale and shopworn and incredibly beyond her twenty-two years. Too many lines in her forehead already. The rough lamenting cough of an old woman. What stabbed me deeply, though, in a place I didn't even know I had, was how much she was Bruce's daughter—the same deep-set brown eyes, the way she cocked her head when she was listening.

"Now don't get any ideas," she warned Bruce within the first five minutes of her arrival. "I'm just here visiting—that is, if you all are up to having a visitor."

"Of course, honey. Any time. You know that," Bruce told her.

It was true—her luggage did appear to suggest only a short visit. She had a small Nike duffel bag, a green backpack, and a ragged blue canvas tote that said *Read: Get Carried Away with a Book.*

"Still traveling light, huh?" Bruce asked her, and all of us knew that he was commenting on more than her luggage.

"Well, you know me," she said, "pack small, think big," then took off her shoes and went upstairs to use the bathroom.

When she was safely out of range, Bruce looked at me, sighed, ran his hand through his hair which is grazed with silver but still as thick as a teenager's, and said, "Here we go, Eileen. Hold on."

Naturally, I thought that *we* was just a manner of speaking, because Lorna, it seemed to me, was Bruce's unfinished business, but that's what is oftentimes so surprising. What at first seems to be someone else's story can suddenly twist and become your own.

⁓⁓⁓⁓⁓⁓

This rocky, ponderosa stretch of the West is actually my third home. First there was Santa Barbara, then Tucson, and after I met Bruce and the flame we created wouldn't die, he moved me here to Colorado with him—long story made short. Instantly, these mountains got all of my respect, but it was the winter—the snow—that thrilled me. I remember my first year here, walking out of Food Warehouse into the first good snow of the season, and after I'd put the groceries in my trunk I sat out on the hood of the car like a crazy woman and let the huge flakes drop softly around me. For years my mother had tried to make me a Catholic, and if Catholics had prayed to snow, in that moment she might have succeeded.

When I arrived home, my hair was in long wet strands and I was shivering, and Bruce asked me if I didn't know when to come in out of the cold. "This might be something you don't understand yet," he said, "but this weather looks just the same watching it from inside." He took a clean towel and wrapped my head. In simple ways, Bruce and I took care of each other, which sounds old-fashioned, but it is the truest form of love that I have ever shared with a man. He bent over and rubbed my feet hard, finally working his way up past my ankles, wandering toward my knees. We stretched out on the living room floor, and with me on top we crashed our way to happiness and exhaustion.

Afterwards Bruce fell asleep as he always does, his foot on top of mine so that we were still two leaves connected, his lips parted as if there was a word there about to be spoken. I lay on my side and watched the snow drifting, piling up around the fenceposts, covering the pines with a dreamy blanket that in a day or two would snap the weaker limbs.

Lorna's favorite color was black. Black worn loosely: an extra-large sweater over black pajama bottoms. Sometimes, black worn skin-tight: a one-piece ebony bodysuit revealing her every shallow breath. Looking at Lorna in an outfit like that was painful—her chest thin and hollow as a bird cage, but it was her hair that Bruce couldn't get used to.

"It's not shaved, Dad. It's crewed. A friend of mine in El Paso did it. Barber clippers and a pair of manicure scissors. You wouldn't believe how heavy hair really is." She bounced her head from side to side, demonstrating the lighter, less burdened Lorna to us.

After she arrived, food was the theme at our house, at least as far as Bruce was concerned. He knows that he's at his best slouched up against our old pine table with a bratwurst or grilled cheese sandwich in his hand, listening intently and shaking his head, every once in a while leaning back in his chair to get a better perspective.

Bruce and Lorna were polite with each other, friendly and talkative, and they were agile, too, quickly skating around the serious talk— Lorna's personal life, her health, her plans for what was out ahead. I stayed out of their way, relaxed in the demilitarized zone of the kitchen, made tuna salad and poured chips into a bowl, opened beers for us and a Coke for Lorna. She didn't want beer or anything that could cloud her mind, she said. She walked over to the window. "It's so gorgeous out there. I want to see it all."

Dorsey Newquist, our neighbor who lives about a mile down the road, would have spit teeth if he'd heard her call this place gorgeous in late November. He had to work it, throwing hay to his cattle early mornings, opening the creek, repairing downed fencelines. Just before lunch not long ago he arrived at the front door, told me to turn my stove off and to grab my gloves and jacket and camera. In his old green International, he drove me out to the far side of Shepherd's Hill, parked at the gate, and then walked me out to the pond.

"There she is," he said. "Eight hundred dollars of drowned prime." He took two butterscotch candies from his pocket and we unwrapped them and put them in our mouths. Dorsey sucked so hard that I could hear the candy clicking against his teeth.

At first, beneath the mirror of ice on the pond, it looked as if a big brown-red blanket had been frozen, but as I stood there and studied it, an ear took shape, a huge marble eye, and then the sorry unsophisticated face of a Hereford. Later I brought Bruce back and showed him, although the water level or some condition had changed and the cow had drifted a little farther out and was harder to see. The next time, when we took Bruce's cousin, Paul, the cow was back near the bank and turned the opposite direction. Jokingly, I hummed the theme to *The Twilight Zone*.

Bruce and I drove out several times in the following weeks and watched the strange migration of Dorsey's cow under the ice—it was one of those oddities of winter which we came to look forward to, like pizza every other Friday night. A couple of times we met Dorsey on the road when we were driving out there. He'd stop and stand at the side of his truck and with his eyes watering from the cold he'd laugh and threaten to get an ice pick and a barbecue and to come with us.

Bruce always said the same thing to him: "We're ready for a party whenever you are."

Lorna didn't want to see Dorsey's cow, though we told her it was a once-in-a-lifetime. "It moves," Bruce told her, "it dances under ice," but we couldn't convince her to take the ride to Shepherd's Hill.

She wrinkled her nose and looked sideways at us. "I'm worried about you two," she said.

"Yeah, I know what you mean," I told Lorna. "I've been worried about your dad for a while," I said, tapping the side of my head, crossing my eyes.

"Huh," Bruce said and danced me backwards to the couch where he pulled me down, tickled and wrestled me until I took back my comment.

When we suggested going to a movie, Lorna didn't want to see that either. "I'm tired of Hollywood. Know what I mean?"

The one thing she did want to do was sleep. We put her in the upstairs bedroom at the end of the hall where she fell unconscious for ten or twelve hours each night, arose cheerily, then fixed breakfast for herself.

"A coma," Bruce said when I mentioned it to him. "A blackout. I've seen it before. Don't worry. She's just had a hard time and has to get caught up with the world again."

Even when she sat on our sofa after ten hours of sleep, though, she was squint-eyed and drowsy, her thin legs drawn up under her, her arms always wrapped around herself—as if she was keeping something in. Or out.

I couldn't imagine what kind of life in El Paso had exhausted her to that point, but there was no way I wanted to ask about it either. Privacy, I told myself, is sometimes the best comfort we can be given.

Midday, she returned to bed. Several times I knocked and then quietly opened the door to check on her. She would be spread over the top of the blankets as if she fainted there, and she seemed so sound asleep that I could easily open and close dresser drawers and the closet without disturbing her.

That's how I found the gun. I was putting a couple of Lorna's clean

T-shirts in the drawer—trying to be helpful—and the gun was right there on top, in clear sight, though it took several seconds for the idea to register. I stood in my tracks, not moving, not really believing what I saw, but my heart was pounding anyway. I watched my hand reach out and then down into the drawer, and when I finally touched it and felt the cold sorrow of that metal and saw the realistic detail of the snub nose, I knew it was no cigarette lighter. Slowly, quietly, as though the gun itself was sleeping, I withdrew my hand, then turned to look at Lorna before I slid the drawer shut.

Out of the corner of my eye, before I had fully turned toward her— I would almost bet my life on it—there was a small quick movement: Lorna's eyes closing. When I looked directly at her, though, some instantaneous wave had passed over her and she was totally still, eyes closed, her head tilted as in loose sleep.

For a second, standing there, I doubted myself, thought I was imagining things, but after I had closed the drawer and quietly left the room and had time to replay the whole scene several times I felt sure about that brief tremor in Lorna.

That night I called Bruce downstairs to the laundry room, and as we pretended to fold clothes I told him what I'd seen. He picked lint from a towel and listened.

"Maybe she needs it, traveling alone the way she does," I said. He nodded his head.

"Maybe she's just used to living in rough places," I told him.

"Not much doubt about that," Bruce answered.

What we couldn't say underneath the bare light bulb that hangs over the washer were the darker possibilities. I could see that Bruce clearly didn't know what to do.

After that I watched Bruce drink double scotches before dinner, pouring the Dewar's with the easy wrist of the bartender that he used to be long before I knew him. There were times when he'd stand at the opened refrigerator and bend down into the milky light, and if I asked what he was looking for, he wouldn't know, there was just something he was craving, and in minutes, he'd walk away empty-handed, frustrated, and shaking his head.

Upstairs, in a corner of our bedroom where Bruce has claimed an old rolltop desk as his headquarters, I started finding pages from a yellow legal pad—Bruce trying to find a place to start with Lorna. Like a nervous freshman about to deliver a speech, he jotted down the words he might use with her. *Lorna, you're my only daughter and I have to tell you that I'm worried.* That would be crossed out, and then, below it: *Honey, I've been through my own rough times and there's not a thing you have to hide from me.* In the corners of these pages were the sad scribbles and aimless marks of someone sifting through what to say to his own daughter.

I'm not a mother. The fact is, motherhood is a romantic notion that my ovaries could not live up to. There's a scientific term for my specific infertility, but I've always just told the men in my life that, internally speaking, I was tied up in knots.

You didn't have to be a mother, though, to sense the awkward vacuum that existed between Bruce and Lorna. They would be together in the kitchen and no matter how close they stood or how relaxed they seemed they were continually on guard. Tiptoeing. Straining. There was no anger, but something worse, because anger is just sparks and fire and in a while it blows itself out. What separated them was cool and more threatening—the product of years of trouble and late night calls and I don't know what else. A bitter divorce with Lorna's mother. Dreams that unraveled. Hormones and bad summer vacations. Bruce had told me long before that he constantly wavered between feeling he had somehow failed Lorna and, at other times, that she had cruelly failed him, oftentimes with enthusiasm—calling him to say she was living in a Jeep or had sold her amethyst so she could go water-skiing in Mazatlán, then spend a month zigzagging across Mexico with her boyfriend.

During Lorna's visit I became expert at tucking myself away, at burying myself in a good book or becoming totally involved with fixing a leaky faucet. I told myself that I was giving Bruce and his daughter the time and space to patch things up, but I could hear them in the next room artfully dodging each other, and sooner or later the TV would come on, the monotone six o'clock news winding its way between them.

<hr>

The first night that Bruce and I slept in the new blue bedroom we could still smell the paint. I told Bruce to breathe through his mouth and also to get his arms around me fast. I wouldn't say that blue is my favorite color, but given the purposes of a bedroom, there's a reason for blue. Try howling. Try two bodies writhing on a Beauty Rest mattress in the rhythmic darkness just before midnight.

Bruce had to remind me, however, that Lorna was just down the hall. "Quiet," he said, and it was the first time in our whole short, wonderful life together that our love had become noise.

<hr>

Hungry elk wandered down from the mountains and gathered in groups of two's and three's in our yard. They discovered the dryer vent on the back wall of our house and stood there to get warm, basking in the sweet, foreign breeze of fabric softener. Curious at dusk, they stood at the dining room window and peered in at electric lights and the quiet chaos of our lives.

Lorna did not believe in God, she told us. She believed in electricity or some such force that held the universe together.

And guns, I wanted to add. *Something small and deadly enough to fit in an evening bag.*

She talked to us while she did a crossword puzzle. "What's a six-letter word that means *to join?*" she asked.

We ran through possible answers until Bruce finally came up with it. "*Solder,*" he said, and cut into a piece of steaming lasagna I had just served. In our household, though, *to join* was not that easy.

At the seventh-grade dance in Grover City, California, my math teacher, Mrs. Wigenstein, made it look so easy. She simply put her hand on the shoulder of some shy boy and her other hand on some girl pressed up hard against the wall and then gently pushed them together, and soon, miraculously, all the seventh graders were waltzing or twisting, some of the less creative falling back on a version of the Virginia Reel we had been taught in PE, but everyone was dancing. We called her "The Matchmaker" and we relied on her back then, but, in fact, Mrs. Wigenstein was just a gray-haired intermediary, something which I evidently lacked the skills for.

Bruce and I turned on the radio, blasted a few of the songs we liked, danced, and tried to get Lorna to join us. She watched us and shrugged, said she was tired. I don't know if it's just that I have especially good ears or if some part of me is curious about other people's business, but two or three times I heard Lorna's muffled crying from upstairs. I guess it was crying—small sobs collapsing into a long low whine. I'd run the dishwasher or turn the TV on, and in a while, halfway up the stairs, I'd listen closely. No noise from her room. Lorna fallen into her hundred-year sleep.

A month passes quickly for someone who is sleeping most of that time, but for those wide and painfully awake it is viciously long and annoying as static.

Bruce, naked as the glorious day he was born, rolled in the snow and groaned with the pleasure of seals and Eskimos. Then he lay still— played dead—and let the cold work up through him.

Ask anybody here and they'll tell you we have a dry cold in winter, which doesn't mean much to me. You still need to stuff newspapers in the sills of the windows that don't shut tight. You still need a hot-water bottle some mornings to thaw the handle of a car door which has turned to stone overnight.

Bruce, however, had a high tolerance for that dry cold. First, he was in the hot tub on our back deck, the steam rising up off the water like vapor from a lost world, every once in a while his foot or arm making a giant splash. Then, it was as if some alarm went off in him. He sat on the top step of the tub for a minute, gained some kind of balance which I can only guess at, and rolled off into the snow, groaning, flashing me the white half-moons of his butt.

Lorna had driven our Jeep into town, and for a few precious hours we were alone.

I knocked on the window, put my hands together like I was praying, and asked for more, but Bruce couldn't hear me.

Dense cold and wet heat—it's a Colorado ritual.

"No," Bruce told me later. "It was just to keep me from going crazy." By that time he was wrapped in a red and black beach towel and was standing in the dining room. He had quit dripping by then. I had taken a kitchen towel and turbanned it over his wet hair and kissed him on the nose, and as I backed away I could see the puzzled look on his face. "Who is she, Eileen? I don't even know who that girl is."

<hr />

Each morning the snow revealed to me the incidents of the night before. I saw where Rainbow, a neighborhood cat, had crossed our deck and, at the edge, left its yellow spray. On a nearby hillside I saw the big, bald lines where neighborhood kids had been sledding days before on plastic garbage bags. A few of the bags were threaded on a bare pine bough at the bottom of the hill, waving in the wind, waiting for when the kids came back for their next run.

Early one morning, though, before I'd had a chance to see anything in the snow, I saw Lorna near the front door quietly putting on her jacket. The skimpy luggage at her feet made her plans clear. Directly up and to the left, I stood unseen on the stairway.

I watched Lorna pull on a pair of gray insulated boots we had bought her. Carefully, as if she were dressing for more than the cold, she wound a muffler around her neck and tucked its fringed ends into her jacket. She pulled an envelope out of her tote bag and walked it to the bookshelves and left it there for us to read—just *thanks* and *so long* and *don't worry*. She pulled on a pair of gloves and opened the door. Even where I stood—safe, distant, a flannel robe around me— I felt the cutting air blow in.

Long story made short: I didn't stop her, didn't say good-bye, didn't wake Bruce so that maybe . . . I don't know. I guess maybe covers a lot of territory. I turned and went back to bed, slipped under the covers where I found Bruce's warm lanky legs, and I fell into the same murky sleep as that little bear under our deck, the one who must have been dreaming of summer and sunshine and something better than pizza to eat.

Later that day, after errands and a long wait at the pharmacy, I drove home, then hurried from the car to the house with my arms loaded— sacks and dry cleaning. I didn't even manage to get the car door shut. When I had unlocked the front door of the house and set down my load, I turned around and started back to the driveway to close the car. There were my purple gloves and scarf that I had dropped onto the snow-covered ground in my hurry from the car. Like a woman who identifies herself with a string of pearls or her ragged kitchen broom, I saw myself in an instant out there—just three small dabs of color on an otherwise endless, frozen plain. Besides its hundred other tricks, snow can do that, can show you in a lightning flash just who you are.

I stood there looking for I don't know how long. Looking and thinking. Thinking and burning.

At first I thought the far-off throttled roar I heard was my pulse pounding in my ears, but the sound slowed and then gathered momentum and then finally crested over on the east ridge. I looked up at a black spot coming closer, weaving, rearranging itself into a two-headed form, the dark green rounded nose of a snowmobile finally visible. I could smell gas and oil and see its foggy gray trail drifting up into pines. It barreled toward me and the two shapes on the snowmobile became people, neighbors—closer and closer—until I could see that it was some snow-masked man driving, and holding on behind him, blonde hair streaming, one of the Ramos twins throwing confetti. They waved at me when they drove by, but I didn't even have time to get my hand up.

Nocturne

~~~~~~

It was a Tuesday night when Maize and I ran out of money in Santa Fe—a place dusty and old and, if you aren't careful, the last place you might visit. We knew that we didn't have much cash left, but it was a surprise anyway to dig to the bottom of my purse and find only a Revlon eyebrow pencil tucked in the bottom folds. Like someone who suddenly finds herself in deep, dark water, I woke up fast. I dumped my purse out on the queen-sized bed and rummaged through the collection of cosmetics and Kleenexes, pens and maps, car keys, paper clips, sunglasses, and lotion. Nothing. Not a dollar bill. Not a quarter. I stood up with just a towel around me and I looked at Maize for what would come next.

Maize, my cousin, was a homewrecker. She was tall for a woman and dark haired, my wingless angel, and wherever she moved, in whatever room, to pick up a magazine or to just stand at the window, she stayed at the center of things while everything else slid to the edges. "Why would a man want salt when he could have honey?"

she would ask me and then fold her legs under herself wherever she was sitting, and for many men, it was just too much. Compulsion, obsession. Wanting what you can't have, which makes you want it more. Maize—a name she had given herself three years earlier in Portland when she found it in a *Farmer's Almanac*—said that she did not make up the rules of life, but that, thank God, she had the brains to break them.

"Now what?" I asked Maize. I had just finished a long, hot shower. I was wrapped in a big white hotel towel, and I didn't need anyone to tell me that what I had been feeling up until that point was happy. Then, while I was digging through my purse for a comb, the facts started to drift and I realized the money was probably gone—blown in the week and a half we had spent in Santa Fe.

It was the first time I had run my course and come out flat broke, scared, and older. Maize never knew any other way to live but like this: on tightropes or where she found easy passage into others' lives. Whether what she had was borrowed, stolen, or given recklessly to her in darkness or over a bottle of booze or out of some weak, twisted passion, Maize made the most of everything. She spent big and looked good. And when the money ran out, as it often did in those days because there was a cycle to it all—getting and spending and laying waste—she fell and fell hard. That time, starting with that Tuesday night in Santa Fe, she took me down with her, my beautiful milk-skinned cousin, chestnut hair, long legs ahead of her time. Her blue eyes were what I thought of then as medicine.

———————

"O.K., Regina" she said. "Relax. Let's do a quick accounting." But in my heart of hearts, if there is such a thing in me, I knew the money was gone. How could it not be? In room 217 of the El Dorado we had temporarily shed our former selves and assumed the lives of queens. Four hundred dollars worth of new lingerie was a reason for being. Once a day we ordered baseball-sized steaks that melted in our mouths. Neither of us cared about jewelry, but in well-made clothes, in leisure, in the wonder of lying naked and watching late-night cable TV we thought that we felt the presence of God. We were astounded to look over and see each other in a two-hundred-dollar-a-night room. Maize would laugh and say that she remembered, but only vaguely, when I was waitressing. I reminded her that somewhere—ten or twenty lives ago—she had driven a school bus, driven it badly, watched while one kid in the back of the bus crowned another with a crescent wrench.

Maize was not easy to upset. She'd had so many ups and downs that they had all become one big movement. So standing there in the El Dorado with the threat of being broke was merely something in the passing for her, some sign that we were now in the middle of things. Maize pulled out her suitcase and tote and casually searched them. She came up with Bill Barnes's Firestone credit card, which she claimed to be an authorized signer for. She held it up, the red and gold plastic which at that moment offered no safety or comfort for me.

"Maize," I said, "that won't buy us food."

"Well, of course not," she told me. "But if the fuel pump goes or a tire shreds, you might just end up thanking me. Well, thanking Bill, actually."

Bill Barnes was an orthopedist who claimed to finally understand the finely woven fabric of his life when he met Maize. "Nice man," Maize had said of him, "but terminal sentimentality. I've seen him cry about the beauty of bathwater."

I looked over at my cousin who sat glamorous and rock hard in the El Dorado. She was wearing a green silk lounging robe—a short little low-cut surprise we had bought a couple of days before.

"O.K. Just let me in on the plans here, Maize," I said, sitting next to the small storm of objects I had dumped on the bed.

From what I knew of her, she never actually thought about money. Her mind worked through parallel subjects: cars, airline tickets, good leather pumps, a nice bottle of Bordeaux that could have easily paid my monthly rent back home in Des Moines. Somehow, she figured a way to these things. She kept her eyes open and jumped at the means made available to her. I had seen men offer their lives to Maize in airports while waiting at the luggage racks or for the rent-a-car. I had watched hotel clerks soften to her, finally writing off her entire bill, suggesting she come back in the spring when the cherries were in bloom or the festival began or the warm, blue sky turned seamless. "Aren't people just the greatest?" she would turn and say to me.

That was one difference between Maize and me. There were about four people in the world that I loved, only a handful that I could tolerate, and everyone else scared me to death. Runaway trains and drunk drivers don't faze me, but put me in a room full of people and my heart starts pounding against my ribs.

There in Santa Fe on that Tuesday night I was looking at Maize, waiting for my cousin, my thirty-eight-year-old madonna of the pick-pockets, to put our world back into place and set it spinning.

"It's not like I just snap my fingers and there it all is," she said to me from across the room. Her green robe was half-unbuttoned. We indulged each other like that. Some pretty flesh. A ginger thigh.

"Well, I didn't expect you to," I told her, "but we're out of money and we're in your territory now."

"Gee, thanks." She bit the edge of her thumbnail. She crossed her legs and tapped a bare foot on the plush, silvery carpet. "Not to worry," she told me. "Look, we're two young, ablebodied women."

Maize had ample practice working through her financial worries. She had stripped several people bare of their savings, cashed in gold Krugerrands, pawned dead women's jewelry, given love and sympathy in return for an almost new Audi. True to her word, she had spent the money and driven the car into the dust. She didn't know that the small red light on the dashboard was an oil warning.

And yet, this is not to say that Maize was all bad. In fact, in those days she was probably at her best—freewheeling, lively, able to carry on a great conversation in a bar. She could talk politics or come to a convincing moment of truth about some great painting. Babbling incoherently, she could fake French or Portuguese for those listening with untrained ears. In those days—in the good days that I remember—she was a beautiful thing to watch, all kidskin and smooth moves. That was before she lost the faith and cut her hair and took a couple of steps down in the world—falling off in Memphis, shoplifting in Detroit.

But on that Tuesday night in Santa Fe, even though we had run up against and hit the wall, Maize still had the faith. She ran out to the parking lot and she spent fifteen minutes searching the car, and when she came back to the room—lo and behold—she had two rolls of nickels and a pocket of loose change.

"Well, my little Fig Newton, oh you of little faith," she said to me, "get your clothes on. I'm taking you out."

Nightlife with Maize. Window-shopping. Driving around with a decent radio station tuned in. A bottle of sloe gin that we pull out from under the front seat of the car, then stopping at a convenience store for lime Icees. "What do you call this drink?" I asked her.

"Sloe gin lime Icee," she said.

"What if it's a cherry Icee?"

"Oh, that's a cherry Rowdy," she said. "Totally different drink, Reg.

I had never been lost and out of money before, driving around in a town that I didn't know, although it was something that happened to me later many times. A seed gets planted. A taste for fine things is acquired. Maize's face and voice, as I remember them, still go straight to my quick.

We were in Bill Barnes's gunmetal blue Volvo station wagon—a nice enough vehicle with cruise control, the car's title in the glove compartment signed right over to Maize. "Hey," she said, "at least we're mobile." I loved the way she held the steering wheel with the flat of her palm.

We dropped into a couple of bars and proceeded to the H Lounge. The bartenders there were shovel-nosed and all business. A few couples danced with the stiff uneasiness of eighth graders. Maize leaned against the bar and scouted. Two drinks and four dances later, a young gallery owner named Tommy Sodoma was eating honey-glazed peanuts out of Maize's hand. And some three hours after that, Tommy was lying in an alley, the rough imprint of a brick still on his forehead. He had proven a little unwieldy back there in the moonlight. When his lack of generosity became apparent, when it was clear that Tommy did not feel like making a donation to us that night, Maize picked up a brick—the only brick, she swore to God, that she ever used—and gave him some much-needed rest right along the hairline.

"Jesus, Maize. Is he dead?" I asked when we returned to the car. Somehow, I couldn't ask that standing over him. There was a thin stream of blood. There were shards of moonlight on the ground. His arms and legs spread out so that he lay big as a Norway spruce.

"Breathe easy, Regina," she said. "He's just taking twenty winks. He's going to have a two-egg hangover tomorrow, though."

As it turned out, Tommy didn't carry enough cash to even get us into the track, and I think Maize regretted having to use that brick. It just was not her style.

～～～～～

Two weeks. Three weeks. I don't know how to tell time when I'm spiraling downward. Maize had my hand and we slept in the back of the car. We washed ourselves over the sinks in dirty rest stops. We had a bar of lavender soap and two big, borrowed El Dorado towels. We took our shirts off and submitted ourselves to cold water and the aftermath.

Maize told me that it would be all right. She kept watch for her next opening, for the place where she would enter another life like a golden breeze, smelling of lavender, ordering with flawless Italian off a menu.

At night, stopped somewhere along the road, we put newspapers up to the car windows. We ate peanut butter straight out of the jar with plastic spoons while Maize told me her life story. Getting and spending and creating the waste that trailed her from Minnesota to the Gulf. "Ever lie on a beach and let the tide roll in around you?" she asked me. "Ever let those dark-skinned waiters walk down and serve you gin and tonics on the sand? Those waiters bend over you, Reg, the glass cold and slick, and it's enough to take your breath away."

We slept a lot for those two or three weeks. Bad dreams. Long, one-way nights, and in the morning, lines of hair-trigger light at the edges of the newspaper. "It's time to get up, Regina," Maize said each morning.

"What for?" I asked.

But Maize always had a way of getting us up and moving. She opened all the car doors and persuaded me with sunlight. She would put her hand on my face and I would recognize that which I could not have, but which I wanted all the more because of it.

Two weeks. Three weeks. And then we separated, figuring one-on-one was easier, surer mathematics. She wanted to go north where Bill Barnes was fly-fishing for the summer. Walking away from me on Market Street, my cousin Maize was both my inspiration and the saddest thing I knew. Hot blood in cold veins—I love her still. She took me down with her for one long, dark month. That was several years ago, but something was planted.

In the years since Maize, I have tried to see things right, but there is never a clear, clean line between what is mine and what belongs to others. In New Ulm, Texas, I spent three weeks in jail, and later— alone, dried out—I borrowed a man and his car in the Carrabassett Valley.

The Uses of Memory

~~~~~~

Netta Cartwright believes these are the things that will bring her husband Franklin back from the dead: thick Velveeta sandwiches, fresh air, plenty of talk and music. She throws the windows open, though it is October in Boise and the smoke-filled breeze whips the lacy curtains, makes them dance in the near-cold. Netta works the radio dial the way other retired women learn to spin the Bingo basket up at St. Mark's on Thursdays—90 percent wrist, 10 percent luck. She turns up the radio's volume when something good comes in: Johnny Paycheck or "The Wabash Cannon-ball." She taps her foot and tries to find the music's rhythm and then tries to pass it on to Franklin.

"You hear that, honey?" she yells, her foot cracking thunder, louder than the radio now.

Carlene, Netta and Franklin's eldest daughter, watches her mother and shakes her head, amazement and disgust and weariness all rolling up into one big ball. "How can you be sixty-three and not know anything?" she asks Netta. Carlene is sorting through a bowl of butter mints, picking out the pinks and slowly eating them.

Netta is too busy to answer or to even listen. She must concentrate on the slippery rhythm, pick it up, then get it all the way down to her foot.

Just an arm's length away from the women, Franklin lies on a bed near the living room window, and in the strictest sense he isn't dead, of course, but he's close enough: low vitals, a complete loss of hair, a mouth that won't form a single word. The left side of his body is soft and slack, useless as a flat tire. Netta has been known to walk right over and smack that arm or give a half-soft karate chop to the withered leg, hoping for even the slightest reaction. She'd appreciate a blink or even a nod from Franklin—thank you—but he just lies there, silent, not even a half-light shining from his old, whiskered face.

Carlene finishes a mint and says to Netta, "There's got to be a special place in hell for you." She moves next to her father, or someone that used to be her father, and lightly strokes his arm: his knuckles, his knobby wrist, then the big, bare root of his elbow.

"Don't get him too comfortable, now," Netta says. "He's just about ready for his bath."

Carlene offers to take a turn cleaning him up, but Netta, as always, says no. To be honest, she doesn't trust Carlene with people. Dogs— yes. People—no. Netta considers her granddaughter Mandy a prime example of how Carlene can take a good person and screw her up, turn her inside out. During all the time that Mandy was growing up, she chewed her fingernails until they had to be iodined and taped; she ate her own long, brown hair; she would sit in front of the TV with her knees up in front of her and suck on them like a child trying to consume herself. Later, on Mandy's small body, the scaly patches of eczema bloomed.

Carlene won't admit to being a poor mother, but Netta thinks she has gotten the message, because after Mandy, Carlene doesn't have any more children; she turns to raising Australian Blue Heelers.

They're a breed that cozies up to Carlene. They lick her face when she bends down to them. They bark and yelp for her when she crosses the yard. Her brown station wagon is scattered with dog kibble, and it doesn't even bother her; she just brushes the driver's seat clean and drives away.

When Netta comes back to the room carrying a big spaghetti pot filled with warm—bordering on hot—water, Carlene quickly steps aside like a pedestrian moving out of heavy traffic. Netta has generously added some of her Peaches and Cream bubble bath to the water, and a small eruption of sweet bubbles glides down the side of the pan and plops onto Franklin's sheet, but Franklin doesn't complain. He hasn't complained about anything in over four months, hasn't fed himself, hasn't been able to stand and take the short stroll down the hall to the bathroom, hasn't even been able to hold his own pruned-up pecker to pee since they put the catheter in.

Months ago, the doctors advised Netta to find a good nursing facility, but all their words were like Chinese to her. She brought him home from the hospital and started at the beginning with him. "Your name is Franklin. You're seventy-two years old. That's the TV the kids gave us a couple of Christmases ago. We can't get channel nine because the damn antenna's no good."

For once, Carlene and Netta agree on something: no hospitals, no old folks' home. Carlene's suggestion is to put Franklin in the living room, right by the window so that he can see out and—she doesn't tell her mother this part—so that he can gently make his escape from Boise and what must be to him a pretty dreary world.

Carlene believes these are the things that will push her father into the next best world: absolute quiet, smoldering pine incense, warmth and coaxing and a big window through which his soul can slip away. She pulls up a folding chair, sits next to his big bald head, and whispers to him: "Look out there and let go, Pop. It's time to let go."

The first time Netta overhears her whispering those things to Franklin she walks up and kicks Carlene's chair, would kick Carlene in that little, skinny, two-bit butt of hers, but she can't get her leg up high enough. "Don't you dare," she hisses at Carlene.

Carlene turns on her mother. "Well look at you, all dressed up like the damn Red Cross! Making him hang on so you won't have to be alone."

Carlene and Netta would gladly part company. They have managed to live as adults in the same city for the past twenty-two years, side-stepping each other except for Christmas and birthdays, but in their plan to bring Franklin home they suddenly need each other. Carlene comes over and spends the days with her father. Netta takes evenings and nights.

Both women are silent as Netta pulls the sheets back and prepares to wash Franklin. It's always a shock—that first, biting look at him: a scarecrow in T-shirt and socks; a pale, bony joke gone bad. Franklin, a licensed electrician for almost forty years, used to have a bumper sticker on his white Ford truck. *Electricians don't grow old. Their wiring just goes bad.* Carlene says that for her that's almost the worst part—the blank, dragged-out look on her father's face.

"It takes time to get well," Netta says, mostly to herself and to the walls. She looks for hope in the smallest of her husband's gestures: a hiccup, a sudden, uncontrolled blinking of the eye. She knows the stories of people who have come crashing up out of comas, big and sleepy as bears at the end of eternal winters.

She begins scrubbing Franklin's feet, starting on his soles, rubbing in much the same way as she cleans her kitchen linoleum. Carlene half expects to see her lather up a Brillo pad.

"Be a little gentle, will you?" Carlene tells her.

"He likes it," Netta says. "He likes the stimulation. It's good for him."

Carlene has to go out and sit in her station wagon to cool down—Netta makes her that mad. She leans her head tiredly against the driver's window. She closes her eyes and breathes in deeply the earthy, tranquilizing smell of her dogs.

~~~~~~~~~~~

Netta is preparing for Halloween, which is in four days. She puts her chubby hand, with four fingers up, in front of Franklin's face. "Four days," she says to him, loud and slowly. "One, two, three, four," she counts, making each finger bob. She gathers brown, crinkly leaves and randomly sprinkles them like fairy dust over the living room end tables. She sets a big, uncarved pumpkin on top of the TV so that the rabbit ears stick up behind it. She rolls Franklin temporarily away from the picture window while she decorates it with packaged cobwebs, then pushes him back in place.

She is surprised at how Franklin fits in with the holiday decor. Paper-skinned and mummy-like, he lies in front of the webbed window, already fitting in, contributing his best to Halloween. Netta can see that. She can see him struggling to come back, to move, to talk again so that they can have those crazy morning conversations that make him laugh and shake his head and threaten to go see if his old girlfriend, Danielle Berry, will take him in. Netta thinks, hell, if it would make him recover any faster, she'd double-time Danielle right over to his bedside, tie her there, feed both of them mashed potatoes and the baby-soft food of recovery.

Carlene can feel Halloween out there, the air thin and solemn, but unlike Netta she just can't get the heart for it. Nothing out of the ordinary decorates her living room. Drake and Faye, her two favorite Blue Heelers, snooze at the end of the Herculon couch, though they aren't really festive in any way, except for their braided brown and orange collars perhaps. Drake's eyes are closed but they twitch, indicating— somewhere—the murky dreams of a dog.

Even though Carlene and her husband Ham have been invited to a costume party, Carlene decides that she won't be anything this year. Last year she was a Viking, and Ham hung a potato six inches off his belt and told everyone he was a dictator. This year Ham has gone down to a local playhouse and rented a King Neptune outfit. For days he has carried his mock trident around the house, goosing Carlene with it, trying to get her in the mood.

"Can't you see I've got other things to think about?" she tells Ham, who, as Neptune, is only momentarily put off.

The fact is, she cannot get her father to let go, despite the incense she burns, despite the calming voice she uses to tell him that everything is okay here, that all of his work is finished, that he can stop holding on. She waits, of course, until Netta has left the house for the morning.

She rummages in Netta's haphazard filing drawer and finally fishes out what she's after. She carries a green vinyl packet marked Riverside Memorial Garden back to her father's bedside. She opens it to a page with a photograph of marble statuary, shows it to him, and reminds her father that everything has been taken care of. It takes Carlene a few minutes to find it on the down-to-scale map, but she finally pinpoints plot 124D, puts her finger on it, and shows her father. "Kinda on the hillside," she tells him, "looking down over the river. Remember? It's real nice. You helped pick it out a long time ago." Carlene hopes that this will be one more string cut for the old man who seems not her father, but only a man using her father's name.

She gets down at bed level and looks right into his face, but it's like peering into a cavern. He looks back at her with the blank, rheumy eyes of sheep or cows, and suddenly she wants it done, she wants to take a kitchen towel and shoo his soul right out the window. "Go on. Bye-bye. Vamoose." She imagines a white steamy haze scooting out the window, then rising higher and higher above the yard, a gauzy hand waving back at her. She knows that absolute relief could come for her in a moment that quick.

Midmorning, Carlene feeds her father applesauce, which is pure torture for her—feeding a man she once thought put the stars in the sky. He would lead her out into the darkness when she was young and they would lean against the house and look up. Holding his cigarette, he would extend his arm up into the blackness until the faraway, orangy end of his Viceroy seemed to burn a star into place. "There. Another one for you," he would say, a sudden twinkling appearing way out there, and even when she was older—a woman lying in Ham's arms, a mother fixing endless baby bottles—the stars, in some sense, were still from her father.

When Netta arrives home for lunch, she wrinkles up her nose, wants to know what that smell is. "Kinda like Pine Sol," she says, looking behind the couch, then lifting the throw pillows.

"It's nothing, Mom. Nothing," Carlene says, knowing that Netta in no way could understand how pine eases and lifts a person from this life.

Netta has enrolled in a morning crafts class at the Y, and Carlene asks her how it was.

"I left at the break," she tells Carlene. "Making grapes out of colored pipe cleaners is not a craft. Here," she says, bends and takes some books from her tote bag. "This is what I did."

She has checked books out of the library. *The All New Book of Muscle Recovery. Better in 30 Days. The Home Care Manual.* The lending period is three weeks, and Netta intends to memorize it all.

Carlene can feel the determined heat rising off her mother. She notices a thin line of perspiration on Netta's upper lip. Under the sleeves of her mother's cotton dress, there are the delicate beginnings of sweat rings. If Netta were not so dominating and petty, Carlene believes, she could feel halfway sorry for her.

All the little packages of saltines around the house, however, are there to remind her who her mother is. Netta, like some bag lady, shamelessly slips the little crackers into her purse whenever she goes to JB's or The Rib House, as if they are as complimentary as match-books. She says it's just automatic for her to take them; it's from the days when she had teething babies to always think about.

"Get over it, Mom. The last time you had a teething baby was more than forty years ago," Carlene tells Netta.

Carlene also notices how her mother slyly stashes away the last little piece of pie or cake or pizza, as if somehow she hasn't gotten her fair share. Weeks later Carlene finds these little treasures still un-wrapped in the back of the refrigerator, mushy as jam and covered with soft, green fur.

"Honest to God," Carlene tells Ham on the night before Hallow-een when he surprises her with a six-pack of Old Milwaukee, "if I start squirreling things away like my mom, shoot me, please. You'll be doing everyone a favor." She grabs a pencil and uses it to open the flip-top can so she won't break her nail. She holds the beer up in a quick toast to Ham, then leans back and takes her first long, cold drink.

"Tell you what," he says. "I'm going to shoot you if you don't get a costume ready for tomorrow night."

Carlene's doorbell starts ringing at twilight the next evening. Gob-lins and rabbits, witches and ballerinas crowd her front porch, then drift noisily away when it is apparent that no one is going to answer. Carlene has exactly seven mini candy bars in a bowl, which means she has popped thirteen of them herself while sitting at the break-fast nook, feeling black and weightless, listening to her doorbell as it becomes one long, fluid ring.

Later, when Ham comes out of the bedroom dressed in a sea-blue off-the-shoulder robe with a cardboard crown barely balanced on his head and the gold trident flaking glitter everywhere, Carlene turns around on her stool, gawks at him, and finally claps. She knows that this is as good as Halloween will get for her.

Although Carlene is dressed in everyday jeans and a shirt when they leave for the party, Ham doesn't say a word, doesn't suggest disappointment in the least. In a tight spot Ham's discretion always comes through. He reaches down and puts his arm around her shoul-der and as they walk toward the driveway they watch a tiny lion scurry down the street swinging an orange lantern, making bright arcs in the night.

On the way to the party, Ham suggests dropping by Carlene's par-ents' house since it is still early. Netta answers the door wearing an apron, the pockets stuffed to the top seams with Sugar Babies and

Atomic Fire Balls. She throws her hands back and cannot stop laughing at Ham, who basks in her attention, strolling this way and that, thumping his trident on the wood floor.

Carlene walks over to her father in his bed. The polyspun cobwebs shimmer in the window next to him. His eyes are open, but she can't get him to look at her, and automatically her hand comes up, she snaps her fingers and softly swipes at his nose, a technique that never fails to get a dog's attention.

Carlene, for the life of her, can't explain whether she is watching a reverie or some tangled predicament. He is down to 117 pounds, his big, bare collarbone holding up the frailest of necks, and still he won't let go. All at once the anger that rises in her is so swift and complete that for a moment she can't get her breath. Her lips part and her shoulders lift two or three inches. She backs away from him, whoever he is, until she feels the chair behind her and sits down. She picks up a *Golf Digest* and fans herself and the air comes back to her in small, bitter waves.

Netta is feeding Franklin miniature marshmallows that night—a Halloween treat, she says—depositing them by two's and three's until his mouth is full. Franklin chews by rote, making a soft white soup which sticks in the corners of his mouth.

By the time Carlene and Ham leave, Carlene has her breath back and is brooding again, ready to wring Netta's neck. She sees that if nothing else works the old woman is bound to keep him alive with sugar.

There is a turkey scare two weeks before Thanksgiving. The news has reported a gross shortage of both fresh and frozen birds, which sends Netta into a tailspin. She hits five markets on her side of town, comes home with three frozen Butterball toms, six pounds of cranberries, enough yams for the block.

When she pulls into her driveway and stops the car, the memories start up, like a tune she can't get out of her head—Franklin bustling out the front door to help her carry in groceries. He'd be peeking in the sacks before he even had them into the kitchen, hoping for licorice or peaches or a dark, resinous bottle of Old Crow. Netta wants him back so bad she can taste it—a shallow sweetness in the back of her throat, a raw craving. She opens the trunk and carries in the groceries herself.

"Want one?" she asks Carlene when she is inside the house, pointing at a turkey.

"What are these?" Carlene is holding up a deck of flash cards. Turkeys and Thanksgiving are lost—a million miles away.

"Oh, watch this," Netta says excitedly, taking the cards from Carlene. She sidles up to Franklin's bed and shimmies a thick hip onto the mattress. She does a quick, fancy card shuffle—something she learned in Atlantic City, turns the pile face up, looks at the top card, then centers it in front of Franklin's face. "Tree," she says, "tree," bending her head forward with each hard *t*.

When there is no response from Franklin, Netta swivels around and says, "It may not seem like anything is happening, but the brain is a sponge, Carlene, and he's soaking up our every word, and when he's good and ready he'll start spitting it all back."

Netta moves to the next card. "Mouse," she says, at least three times, pointing to the picture, which simply infuriates Carlene.

Before Netta can get to the next card, Carlene stops her. "Okay, okay," she yells, "that's enough." Her arms are stiff at her sides. Her hands are balled into the tight fists that have started to dominate her life. "How can you do this?" she asks her mother. "How can you humiliate him? He is not getting better."

"Well, I'm glad to hear you have a medical degree now, Miss Smart-Ass," Netta shouts. She turns her back to Carlene and stops the argument flat, her usual tactic.

Before she really has time to think about what she is doing, Carlene glides past her mother and scoops up the thick, blocky, first-grade cards right out of Netta's hands. She walks to the front door and opens it, then pushes back the screen and throws the whole stack, Frisbee style. They catch the air and go down slowly. The rose card spirals. The hat card catches high in the privet. The zebra almost touches the ground and then is caught up again and carried to the neighbor's yard.

Netta puts her hands on her hips and walks to the door and both women stand there looking out at the white whirlwind of litter across the brown grass. Sorrow has hammered its way so far into their chests that a moment like this—a sudden mess, something that now has to be picked up off the lawn—is strangely welcome in their lives.

Carlene turns to her mother and says that, yes, she will take one of the turkeys.

<hr />

Each evening, in the voice of a librarian that she once knew from Okinokee, Netta reads the newspaper to Franklin. She polishes the vowels, repeats any important names, and in general tries to make sense of the world to Franklin.

"Ice Palace Collapses" she reads to him, an article sadly detailing how the local Jaycees' icy Christmas wonderland melted due to a puzzling electrical short. "In only a few hours," she reads, "the life-sized ice reindeer were reduced to winter slush." She abbreviates the articles, tries to keep the news short and to the point for Franklin, who dozes often and unexpectedly. She is especially on the lookout for uplifting news—lottery winners, dogs that roam two thousand miles to find their owners, job openings down at the canning factory. She doesn't actually see a smile on Franklin's face, but for a moment his cheeks seem to draw up, he seems to want to smile, and certainly that counts for something.

Another thing that Netta is convinced he enjoys is the family pictures. From the attic, she has brought down several old albums and she is teaching him his family all over again. "You have two brothers, Franklin. Their names are Clarence and Reed. Clarence is in the nuthouse, I'm sorry to say, and Reed still drives for Greyhound Bus."

She points and turns the album pages slowly, lingering on some, getting teary-eyed over long-gone uncles and the way that all the couples loop their arms loosely, though the knot between them is tied deeply elsewhere. When she grows tired, she moves Franklin over and climbs up onto the bed with him. He has blankets up to his chin. He has lost his eyelashes and his eyes have receded back into the sockets, dark pools with no understanding. She lays her arm over him and thinks of peas in a pod, buttons in buttonholes, her crochet hook with the thread wound tightly around it.

That's how Carlene and Ham find them when they arrive at the house bringing the surprise three-foot spruce. Carlene walks over to the bed, appalled, her mother dwarfing her father as she has never seen before. And Netta's freckled arm pinning Franklin as sure as ground ropes.

When Netta wakes up, Carlene wants to give her hell, but she steadies and calms herself and gives Netta the Christmas tree she and Ham have brought instead. "See how it's nice and full all the way around," Carlene says, holding the top of the tree and spinning it so that a few dry needles go flying.

The tree sits there undecorated, untouched. Day after day Netta often looks over at it and Christmas has never seemed so small to her. The tree barely reaches to her waist, won't hold more than a handful of ornaments. It's not like the trees they used to have—bushy ten-footers, trunks thick as a thigh.

In the weeks before Christmas, in the stone-cold winds that sweep down from the north, Boise gets lively. Rum-filled carolers totter from house to house. Quiet holiday cocktail parties mushroom into entire block parties. Stray crepe paper and tinsel blow down the streets in the early mornings. The mood infects Netta and even Carlene. Netta gives herself a holiday goal: to get Franklin to sit up. She starts out small—five minutes at a time—the surgi-bed cranked up and

Franklin secured with a soft rope of dish towels. His head droops miserably to one side or the other, but Netta knows she can't have everything all at once. When she has him up, she sets an empty coffee cup on his lap, stands back, and the results are impressive. To her, enough hope, an empty cup, and their lives are back again.

Carlene doubles her efforts on the days she spends with her father. She gives him short, hushed pep talks: "Go on. There's not a thing to be afraid of." She turns his head to the side so that he has to see out the window, so that he can't avoid the broad, welcoming sky. Cones of incense burn around him, the sweet smoke nudging him away.

What is usually a flurry to get the shopping done and the gifts wrapped becomes just Netta and Carlene moving frantically around the old man, cranking his bed up and down, bringing their separate messages to him: stay, go. Netta plies him with raw cookie dough and spoonfuls of half-cooked divinity, sings for him and dances—as well as she remembers how. Carlene brings him clear broth and melba toast and lays a warm cloth on his forehead.

It's finally Ham who decorates Netta's Christmas tree when he sees it won't get done otherwise. He goes for something novel—he can see that this is no ordinary year, no run-of-the-mill Christmas. At a nearby Sprouse Reitz, he chooses plastic chili peppers and little white lights. He is slow and meticulous with the spruce, taking all of an afternoon to arrange it.

Ham gathers everyone that night for the tree's unveiling. He springs for pizza, and even before the tree is lighted Netta's house is full of the celebratory smell of pepperoni, rich and spicy. Drake has been allowed to come; he sits at Carlene's side and gulps the oily pepperonis that she tears off her pizza for him.

When they gather in the living room for the lighting ceremony, Netta has a surprise: she has managed to drag Franklin into a chair and prop him up with pillows. Most of his body is still uncooperative and any similarity he has to a man sitting in a chair is coincidental, but Netta doesn't care. She thinks that from where they have been it's a step forward.

Carlene has to bite her lip when she sees him. She decides not to interrupt Ham's program, but as soon as it is through, she intends to march Netta out to the kitchen and shake her out of the tree she's been living in all these months.

Ham turns off the overhead light. He feels his way back along the wall, bends and plugs in the tree. His work has paid off. The spruce looks larger, its boughs suddenly thick. The chilis hang in red, open-heart clusters and there, on the tree, become the essence of Christmas itself. The hundreds of tiny white lights pulse and glitter and shoot through the room.

For minutes, all of them are still and transfixed, caught in their private hopes and remembrances as they stare at the small, brilliant tree. Slowly, Carlene looks around and then Netta, and they see the old man with the white light from the tree shining right through him—his big head as clear as an aquarium, his eyes blinking as if on a timer. Drake gets up from the rug where he's been lying and barks twice at Franklin, not sure what he's looking at.

All at once Netta has to sit down—her legs are shaking, her chest heaving, and her first thought is, she hopes Carlene is happy. There's Franklin, empty and transparent as a bread wrapper, sitting up in his living room six days before Christmas. Just half a man, Netta knows, which, of course, is no man at all.

Carlene stands there and pulls her sweater tighter and tighter around her. She can see that the window has worked, that her father has been gone for at least weeks, maybe months, but that Netta has won her claim, too. Like a salty rind, Franklin's body has stayed to find its way through Valentine's and Easter and beyond to who knows when.

Ham messes with the top of the Christmas tree and rearranges a couple of lights. He turns to Netta and Carlene and wants to know who'll put on the star.

Exactly Where I Am

I don't know where I am—on the porch, at the screen door, standing on the backyard walkway—but I know that I'm there when Daddy and Uncle Gill find RayAnn's fingers in the grass. Where I am standing seems less important than the way the flashlight steals the grass from the night, studies it slowly, then names it green. Daddy holds the light and Uncle Gill bends from a lifetime of factory work into the grass for his daughter's fingers— RayAnn who has cried all the way to the hospital, her hand wrapped in what was a clean bath towel. I'd call her a big, fat crybaby, but I'm half-sick myself, wherever I am—porch, screen door—the half-grown daughter of another factory worker, the one who holds the flashlight and yells at me to get back into the house. "Mind your own business," he says. "Go watch the kids."

I think my cousin's fingers are my business. I think my cousin's fingers, strangely enough, are the proper study of this night. She didn't even realize they were gone until her brother started screaming. She had run past the metal storage shed, and on the torn corner where Uncle Gill had accidentally backed the Buick too fast two winters ago, she had caught her hand, the metal sharp and cold and always just beyond Gill's fixing. That's constantly the way it was—more to get done than there were hours in the day: the storage shed, the roof, the upstairs window. In the garden nearby, potatoes swelled, then rotted in the ground.

And then so fast that even a moment seems too long an explanation, RayAnn's fingers were gone and she was running past the tree, beyond the gladiolus to the rock driveway. Slender and turning dark as peach pits, two fingers lay in the cool, thick grass. Cory screamed with every ounce of breath in him and pointed, not at the driveway as we first believed, but at the setback in our lives that night: RayAnn's hand in its new shape.

Before pain or shock or understanding, before RayAnn's shorts streak completely red, I know where I am. Barefoot and half-grown at Uncle Gill's birthday and these are the two families of factory workers in a summer yard and when we sing we are thieves and castaways. Our rendition of "Happy Birthday" is the one where everyone draws the last word out, fighting against breath, letting the trick candles have their time to pop and spark. Gill closes his eyes when he makes a wish. That deep, that strong. One layer of chocolate and one layer of white to please everybody, my Aunt Jen says, and we are pleased, cake in our hands, a wish, the box fan whirring in a kitchen window.

My uncle is not even forty the night he finds his daughter's fingers in the grass after we have sung to him with the voices of country radio where all the songs are sad or humbled or on the very verge of drifting. Daddy takes the flashlight down off a pantry shelf, and Gill kneels near the shed out of necessity, and the light falls between them, cold and pale as dishwater. The doctor has sent them back here to work the grass, to hold the light, to grow old, and to be sung to. I have been born to watch the kids, though instead I am watching two men from some place beyond my memory, beyond the rock driveway.

The TV is on in the background and in front of me is a moment that cannot be relieved by time or surgery. Gill takes his handkerchief and wraps the fingers like small mementos which he and Daddy will drive through twenty miles of a summer night to deliver.

My business takes me out there—porch, screen door, walkway— to watch what happens after a party when the men are given the odious task of picking up. They search the grass quietly because they know how to get a job done, having been trained at J & B Manufacturing. Gill is in Quality Control and Daddy operates a lathe, and together in the yard their figures speak of labor that takes ten years off their lives. Inside the house their kids eat ice cream from paper cups and watch TV.

My uncle's handkerchief could be the center of this night, and the grass, the bare feet, the cake, the wish, the kids' voices doubling and tripling into a choir, even summer as it is threaded through the box fan in the kitchen window, are all periphery.

"Go watch the kids," Daddy says. He doesn't return the flashlight to the shelf, and when he backs the car from the driveway, my uncle holding the only darkening gift that will matter in his life, our dusty world is caught in headlights: two seconds of a house, a flash of tree, the tremor of pink gladiolus.

I'm left with the kids. I'm left tall for my age, a gunnysack figure and the disposition of a handful of weeds. *Pretty* is not a word that I think of here. I don't know the word for being young and tall and in the dark, half-woman, half-sick.

Left with me in charge, the younger kids drag the party on, unwilling to let the night go, reluctant to believe that anything has an end. They finish the ice cream and throw their cups out the window. They box each other, run the stairs for fun, appoint a temporary king, gather sheets right off the beds to make a tent. I consider using brute force. I consider RayAnn crying the twenty miles of a summer night, Mama and Aunt Jen in the back seat clutching their purses. What more can they do?

Certainly, I am not the center of this night that has started with a party and ended with a ruined towel. Looking at the blue-black sky, it seems it's nobody's birthday, though we have sung earlier, we have howled while the candles burned their broken flames. Thus the night is doubled, tripled, more voices than bodies, the sky more blue than black.

When I close my eyes, it is not to make a wish, but to forget the cups thrown from the window onto the lawn. The paper cups are not the center of this night, though for a moment they threaten to be. The summer yard—that deep, that strong—is its own character in this story where my cousin's second and third fingers have been lost quick and clean and she stands without pain at the driveway. Everyone else who ever matters is standing there, too: Mama in a dress two sizes too big; Daddy like a dark, stormy block of wood; my sisters who will end up making the prettiest brides and my brother already with his dreams of big money.

Losses and small parties—all of this happens in the two seconds of my growing up. On the porch or at the screen door, I am standing half-woman in the dark. Standing all-woman in the dark is not much different.

Frog Boy

~~~~~~

Rocky Davis is all hands and eyes. Big hands—state of Texas hands. Shoulders broad enough to suggest his first good sport coat. He is already wearing size 10 men's shoes, and since last Thursday, Rocky has been on fire. It started as a hot, hopeless weight in his chest and then suddenly blew wide open, his hair smoldering, his arms and face so flushed that twice his father, Wade, gently reaches over to him, puts a cool square hand on his son's shoulder, and tells Rocky to go shower.

"Christ, the kid just can't stand this heat," Wade says, shaking his head. Rocky is his best son, his only son, the big sleepy kid who doesn't look a thing like him.

It is late August in Tucson and each day the temperature slowly bulldozes upward to 107 or 108. Everywhere in the city, people have lost their patience for summer, for the flies littering windowsills like shiny black tacks, for the steaming sidewalks, and the small patchy Bermuda lawns turned brown, the gardenia and palm leaves limp as day-old sandwich makings. Some of the small restaurants have even closed for the month and put signs in their windows: *Too hot to cook.*

Rocky just stands there a few moments, as if his father's words take that long to unspiral and plant themselves. Finally, he heads for the shower, taking his time, dragging those Texas hands of his along the dresser until they encounter his father's credit card there. One flick of his wrist and the shiny red plastic is gone.

Rocky doesn't like being told what to do. He'd rather choose. He'd rather live in a free universe, he says.

"Rocko, my boy," his father tells him, "this is about as free as it gets."

Wade resumes eating his Baby Ruth, which is breakfast that morning. Three fingers on his right hand wear the delicate brown signature of chocolate, until he licks them and begins to look for the opened sack of Cheetos which he knows is somewhere nearby, and probably under some clothes there's a minibag of Oreos. Usually Rocky and his father don't eat like this, but they're on vacation and whatever rules composed their former life in Denver have been erased.

In the big white tiled bathroom of the El Conquistador Hotel where they are staying, under a stinging spray of water, Rocky stands still and counts to three hundred, which is longer than he has ever stayed in a shower before. It's dangerous in there, he thinks—a bad place to be in an earthquake, the plumbing folding permanently up around him like a tiled coffin.

Steam billows around him and the plastic shower curtain rustles in a warm synthetic breeze. He crosses his arms and buries his hands in the smooth, slick pockets of his armpits. He tucks his head and lets the water pour down over him—a rain, a flood taking off his first skin and leaving him the raw thirteen-year-old that he is: long thin legs interrupted by knees the size of salad plates and, recently, tufts of dark jungled hair down there.

He knows beyond a doubt, there in the shower with his hands safely put away, that he loves her: Ellen Castillo—his father's girlfriend—the woman in the adjoining hotel room who has touring maps of

Tucson spread around her, blue X's marking the sites that they will probably visit: the air museum, the desert zoo, the mission. A tortilla factory. A designer underwear outlet.

Rocky doesn't care where they go as long as it's with her. Africa. Iceland. He and his father were backpacking in the rainy mountains of Tennessee two years ago and he thinks he could probably even stand that again, if she were there, despite the grenade-sized mosquitoes and the sloppy one-pot meals cooked over a campfire.

In a few minutes, his father is there knocking on the bathroom door, telling him that they're waiting. "Hey, buddy, let's get going," he says.

Wade Davis's voice dulls as it passes through the door and into the steam where Rocky, now standing with a soft white towel around him, hears only a low frequency disturbance—a bug, a bee, something mildly whining out there on the landscape of the tan carpet. He reaches for his T-shirt and shorts and smells them before he dresses: wind, fading fabric softener, and the steely edge of that morning's earlier sweat—the second since he has awakened.

Last year in August on their annual vacation they had flown to Seattle where he didn't sweat at all, he and his father and Eve Resnick—the woman back then, someone who had insisted on high heels, though she couldn't walk in them. She teetered down Pike Street. Packed into Spandex pedal pushers, she wobbled up the long sidewalk leading to the Space Needle. Rocky looked the other way or tried to make it seem he was with another family. He crowded up behind two dark beanpole brothers, hoping to make it look like three. Down on the wooden wharf, as a rusted tugboat pulled up to dock, Eve had finally caught a heel and fallen, and for the rest of the trip she wore scabbed-over knees and consoled herself with tall gin and tonics. Mai tais. Red table wine.

Rocky notices that Ellen Castillo wears blue tennis shoes or sandals with lots of tiny straps across the toes. On the first day of their vacation, which was last Thursday, at a Denny's where they were eating lunch, Rocky discovered Ellen's feet, and the match was lit; the fire in him began, though his understanding of that fire was elementary still: heat, dizziness, a pulse hammering in his ears—he was not even sure it was his own. Back in Denver, he had only briefly seen Ellen, but now, in the long sunblasted days of what seemed like the other side of the world, he was getting to know her, or at least beginning to become attuned to her every move.

That day at Denny's, wayward and without cares and lugging big tote bags, they all ordered just what their hearts told them. Wade ordered a shrimp cocktail and a hot brownie sundae, which he intended to eat in reverse order. Ellen ordered the peach melba plate. Rocky opted for just an order of French fries, but when they finally arrived he found that he had no appetite. Food seemed boring, a waste of time when Ellen was sitting there in what smelled like a cloud of orange or sweet lemon.

"Gotta keep your strength up on this trip," Wade reminded his son when he saw him fidgeting and the fries untouched. "We're going to be in high gear," he said. "We're going to be seeing everything there is to see in this town."

Wade arrives in a new place—Tucson, Tennessee, wherever—with all the spirit of an invading general. He carries guidebooks and maps and has a hit list of places to definitely see. For months before his vacation, he falls asleep on the sofa each night with a Fodor's travel book opened on his chest, and it is as if, during those naps, he absorbs the intricacies of a given place—falls in love with the names of unseen streets and rivers and mountains.

During lunch at Denny's, Ellen had her legs crossed, her right foot sticking out from under the table. Rocky had never really noticed a foot before, let alone fallen in love with one. Her painted toenails made him feel inexplicably happy. Across each, she had pasted a glittery gold zig-zag so that every toe ended in a tiny bolt of lightning. A sizzle. A pop. He noticed that her foot was clean and tanned, that her toes curled or pointed up when she laughed or leaned forward to make some teasing remark to Wade. The arch was high and white, a secret place. Her small bare ankle bone pushing up under the skin made him sigh, which in turn caused Wade and Ellen to look up from their plates at him.

"What?" his father asked him.

Uncomfortable, Rocky shrugged and scratched his ear.

In what seemed like a minute to Rocky, Ellen's melba plate was gone and there was only a smoky green lettuce leaf left on the thick white china. She looked at her watch and tapped its face. "Hey guys," she said, "are we going to spend all day eating lunch?"

While she waited for Wade and Rocky to finish, she reached up and behind her and examined a heavy woven valance hanging in the window. Ellen is a drapery consultant and says she is in love with the feel of things—burlap, sateen, canvas. A good brocade makes her dizzy. Silk—good silk—she says you won't find in this country. Wherever they go, she has her hand out in front of her and opened, like a blind person who is searching a path, but instead she is registering the thread weight and gauge of chairs and curtains, anything covered in fabric that comes her way.

Rocky is not at the point where he can actually look at Ellen's face and listen to her. Looking at the door to the Denny's rest room, however, was safe. Looking out the window was momentarily calming. The windows were tinted, but even so, he had never seen sunlight that savage.

When the three of them were almost out the restaurant door, Rocky had a flash, did a quick backtrack to their table, snagged the lettuce leaf from Ellen's plate, and put it in his pocket.

～～～～～～

In a sky-blue rented Mustang with the top down, Rocky's father drives faster than he probably should. Rocky sees cactus and palo verde zip by, long adobe walls, and the vast brown plate of the desert. In the wind that hits his face and batters his hair, he smells sun and exhaust and the brown coyote smell of dirt. He can't see the speedometer from where he's sitting in the back seat—slumped in the left corner, sitting on one crushed leg, leaning into the plush upholstery for strength.

In the front seat, Wade has placed one hand casually on Ellen's neck. Slowly his index finger moves up and down across the skin just below her ear, making a tiny but suggestive path. Rocky homes in on the hand and can't let go. His shoulders tighten and he can clearly taste the spicy composition of last night's food.

The three of them are headed for a movie set west of Tucson. Wade leans his head to the right and half-yells back at Rocky. "Isn't this great? Getting to see a movie being made and everything?"

Ellen swivels toward the stick shift. "Yeah," she says into the wind. "We're just too lucky, aren't we?"

Rocky can't quite make out what either of them is saying. It's not just the speed and rushing air that distort their voices, but the fact that Rocky's ears are half-plugged. He sees their mouths move. He hears a droning. Every few seconds, an understandable word flies, comet-like, at him: "everything," "lucky." Like a foreigner, he scrambles to patch together the conversation.

For the first time in his whole life, his father's hand bothers Rocky, actually repulses him. Up until now, it has mostly been a good hand—generous, caring, luminous in the dark. Now, it seems to Rocky, the knuckles are too big; the nails, squared-off and thick and almost yellow. He wishes Ellen would say something about it, would complain that the hand is too hot and heavy, would squirm in her bucket seat until she cast his father off and he had two hands on the steering wheel again. Rocky thinks that for once his father should be concerned with safety.

About ten miles out of town where a graveled road takes off from the highway, Wade makes the turn to the movie set a little too sharp and the three of them lurch toward the right. Ellen and Wade laugh as if a car and a roller coaster are supposed to have something in common. Rocky, irritated, hunkers down lower in his corner, trying to keep from sliding across the seat.

When the car finally stops in the dusty parking lot and Rocky tries to stand, he finds that the folded leg he has sat on is numb. Ellen and Wade hurry across the dirt lot and into a huge, abandoned machine shop where the movie is being made. Rocky follows more slowly, slightly limping, trying to shake the pins and needles loose.

The film is not yet titled. In it, an alien of unknown origin—masterminded by two special effects men—confronts a woman at an old rundown desert motel. On the set, there's a bright pink neon sign rigged up—Tumble Inn—buzzing and half-lit. Portable lights are set up everywhere, creating a sharp blue-white halo that appears thick as cigarette smoke. A man wearing a cap with horns sprouting out the sides is being raised up above the set on a noisy black crane. He is obviously unhappy—yelling and pointing and shaking his head. "Fuck you, Louie, just fuck you," he hollers from about twelve feet up.

Ellen can't believe how skinny the actress is. "You can't tell me that's attractive," she says quietly, standing on her toes for a better view. She turns to Wade. "Is that attractive?"

Wade shakes his head no and puts his arm around her shoulder. Ellen smiles and settles herself into the tan muscled groove of his bicep. At home in Denver, he and Rocky share a Joe Weider weight set, and Wade has been making good progress, though Rocky finds the weights boring. He'd rather lift one of the wrought-iron kitchen chairs over his head, spin it like the people from the Moscow Circus who could make a whole ladder of spinning chairs, or he'd rather see, with just one leg, how far he can push the bulky gray sofa. Besides, Rocky lately finds his muscles ungovernable. Right in the midst of flag football, for instance, or a neighborhood game of catch, a leg cramp rivets him to the ground where he clutches the grass embarrassingly.

At the movie set Rocky watches the show of affection between his father and Ellen—pats and rubs and long full-body presses, the quick birdlike kisses of the newly in love—and at the same time he somehow watches the filming. He can see both up and down, far left and far right. It is as if his field of vision has quadrupled. His brown eyes flick and rotate, finding both the obvious and the hidden: a star-shaped mole on a woman's neck, a hole in the sleeve of a cameraman's shirt. When Rocky can't stand it anymore—the lights, the swirling movement, the actress's face being dabbed with sponges, his father pulling Ellen closer and closer—he heads for a portable Coke stand back by the entrance.

He gets in line and starts to dig in his pockets for change. His left hand comes up and in it is shredded paper, a button, a few twists of lettuce and orange peel. He stares at the contents of his pocket, confused. The line keeps shortening until there is only one man in front of him. Rocky hurriedly feels for coins in his right pocket, but everything there is vague and unfamiliar, the warm dark terrain of someone else's clothes. The man in front of him is reaching up onto the counter now for a red and white paper cup. The girl selling Cokes brushes hair from her eyes and starts to look back in the line.

Rocky feels the pressure of the moment as a huge bubble that works its way up from the bottom of his stomach and lodges in his throat, threatening as a chicken bone. Even if he had the money resting coolly in his hand, he knows he couldn't say a word. The Coke girl, tired and bored, would lean forward, waiting for his order, the mounds of her small earthy breasts rejoicing momentarily from the top of her halter.

Rocky slips out of line and shoulders his way to the rest room. The one sink in there has been torn inches away from the wall and a chipped green welder's tank temporarily props it up. A silvery stream of water snakes down the wall from a joint in the plumbing. Rocky pulls the water lever on and dunks his head, and when he finally straightens back up the water runs down his neck and soaks the top of his shirt. Drowns him. Saves him. In four days, he hasn't felt this good.

Wade is browsing at the souvenir stand—a wooden cart loaded

with T-shirts and cactus highball glasses—and when he sees Rocky standing over by the extras, wet almost to the waist with his dark woolly hair slicked back, he stops and looks again. "Criminy," he says when he's standing at Rocky's side, "I almost didn't know you. What happened?"

Rocky doesn't know how to explain much of anything. Ellen strolls up behind Wade, and Rocky certainly doesn't know how to explain this feeling he gets when she's near: his arms and legs become weighted, his throat tightens to the width of a string. The bare blue heat intensifies between his legs. Yesterday his shoes would not stay tied in her presence, and if it had not been for the egg-frying heat of the concrete, he would have thrown them away.

Ellen looks sleepily around the movie set and says that, all in all, she's disappointed. "To tell you the truth," she says, "I'd rather go to a theater and watch a movie than see it being made."

Wade raises his hand in agreement, votes yes for Ellen.

They look at Rocky, but his answer has darted completely away from him, slippery and unreliable, and when his lips open, when he tries to coax it out, a small low-pitched belch is all he can muster.

Ellen giggles and Rocky thinks it's the sound of glass and silver and sunlight falling.

Wade rubs Rocky's head and smiles, and instantly, with a fierce and nauseating instinct he's never felt before, Rocky's hand closes tight at his side, as if he were grabbing onto and then raising a two-by-four against his father.

Just before they leave for the Sonora Desert Museum, Wade discovers his credit card gone. He hits the side of his head a couple of times like he's just come out of a swimming pool and needs to empty an ear. "Now where in the hell would I have left that?" he asks himself. He's mad and worried, which Rocky finds a strangely satisfying combination.

Ellen starts to work their way backwards for him. "Let's see. We were in the hotel café for breakfast this morning. And last night . . ."

In Rocky's room, behind the swivel stand of a 21-inch color TV, back where no right-minded maid would ever clean, there is a collection of valuables. Wade's sunglasses and electric razor. Now the credit card. Rocky knows that he should feel ashamed, but that's a feeling he can't get inside of and wear anymore. It's like last year's T-shirts—too small, too tight at the neck.

Wade calls and puts a stop on the credit card, and then, not to be deterred, they drive to the desert museum.

Ellen is dressed in green—green shorts, green top. If she were any more green or beautiful, Rocky knows that it would drive him mad, that he would climb the thick cyclone fence and join the pack of gray wire-haired javelinas they are watching. Actually, there's not that much to watch. The javelinas are woven among the boulders of a gray concrete wall. They are facedown in cool dirt, sleeping in deep ovals of shade.

"They've got the right idea," Ellen says.

"Yup," Rocky adds, and it's only a small word, but he soars with confidence. He feels himself smile, his back arch a little. He bites at his thumb and looks down to make sure his fly is zipped.

They move on toward the porcupines. Ellen leads the way. She carries the map and easily decides everyone's destiny. Neither he nor Ellen nor his father can find the porcupines within their enclosure. The three of them lean their faces up to the fence and scour the trees and around the rocks, but can't sight any of the dark barrel bodies.

Warm and frustrated, Wade volunteers to run for snacks, and then it's just Ellen and Rocky walking along a dirt path toward whatever animal comes next. Marsupial. Primate.

It is only midmorning, but already the air is thick and dry as rope, leaden to the taste. People stroll by in clothes that have been cut up for the weather—sleeves and legs and shirttails are raggedly cut off. Parents stop to swathe babies in sun block, then turn and dot each other's shoulders.

Rocky wears a black and white striped legionnaire's hat that his father bought for him the day before in a surfers shop. "Keep the sun off your head," he told Rocky, and for a while Rocky was irked—more instructions—but actually Rocky likes the way the long flaps off the back of the hat flutter against his neck.

He looks up and the cloud-streaked sky is bone pale and beneath it Ellen's hair is streaming with sunlight and the sweet powdery smell of shampoo. She turns the map sideways and reads the fine print that details the petting zoo. Rocky is engrossed with her every move. It seems that he is seeing the small, everyday movements of a human for the first time. She pushes her sunglasses up onto her hair and then squints at the map. She cocks her head to the right and studies.

Then, in the distance where a group of shaggy cigar-colored camels are bunched together, Rocky spots his father holding a big cardboard snack tray, and he makes a split-second decision. He guides Ellen to the right, just nudges with his shoulder, and amazingly she doesn't even look up from the map. She veers softly right, and they weave strategically among other zoo-goers, then head toward the big cats and the elephant. Rocky doesn't remember what all they see on this loop, but Ellen reads to him and points and makes the morning alive. His skin crackles. His heart tentatively climbs back into his chest where it rustles and whirrs.

Rocky doesn't wear a watch, so he doesn't know how long it is before Wade, sweaty and winded, finally meets up with them in the Reptile House. The ice in the drinks that Wade is carrying has completely melted. Cheese nachos tumble one by one off the cardboard tray and the orangey topping oozes over his thumb.

"Hey, Rocko," he says, "didn't you see me back there? Where in the heck have you guys been?"

"Everywhere," Ellen says, waving the map. "Give me a Coke. I'm dying."

There is a strong sour odor in the Reptile House and the first thing Rocky does is drop back from Wade and Ellen, lift his arm, and smell to see if it's him. Rocky doesn't know what to expect out of himself anymore—what strange pink appendages might protrude, what swampy smell might emanate. When he checks out all right, he lowers his arm and hurries ahead.

Ellen practically has her face against the glass of a chamber where a long bright-green snake is wrapped next to an almost perfect replica of itself—a dark recently shed skin. She puts her finger against the glass and taps lightly. The snake is frozen and only the thread of its tongue flicks the stagnant air. Rocky doesn't like watching the snake. He chooses a bark-skinned lizard in a tree doing what looks like push-ups. Wade shakes his head and moves toward the exit. He says he has a bad case of heebie-jeebies.

That's the way that Rocky ends up alone with Ellen in the Reptile House, going from glass to glass, hardly breathing at all, staying the whole time within a foot of her shoulder.

⁓⁓⁓⁓⁓

There are huge propeller-sized fans blowing everywhere around the tortilla factory. The deep, sorrowful smell of grease spreads through the whirring air of the fans, though Josephina, the factory tour guide and a former masa-maker herself, does not refer to it as grease. "Shortening," she says, her accent hardening the *t* and *n*'s, making the word sound like some exotic ingredient. All of the workers wear nets on their heads, spidery black webs that flatten their hair similarly. The edges of their oversized white cotton aprons wave slightly from the fans, and to Rocky these people look like ghosts as they stand solemnly here or there to catch a breeze.

Ellen must feel the tortillas, of course. Josephina says yes, by all means. Ellen picks one up and holds the soft gold and brown specked treasure up to the light and it becomes a round opaque window. Soon there is flour on her fingertips and a white iridescent smudge on her face. Wade walks up to her, licks his finger, and rubs it over the spot on her cheek. In an instant Rocky knows how it feels to have his chest crushed, though he realizes it isn't much of a chest yet—bony, hairless, white.

Rocky pushes ahead to the sales office where the tour will end. He sits in a brown molded plastic chair and stews while he waits for the rest of the group. With one foot, he kicks the sole of his other shoe until that foot throbs, but it is a disconnected pain—just a steady chain of blips on a machine somewhere.

The tour group arrives sampling bits of rolled tortillas, powdered sugar and honey on their hands. Wade saves some for Rocky, but he doesn't want any. He shakes his head and moves next to the air-conditioning unit set in the wall. The icy air pours over his arm and even whispers to him.

Wade wants one evening alone in Tucson with Ellen. "You don't mind, do you, Rocko?" his father asks him when they're back at the hotel. Wade has stopped and bought himself a disposable razor; he thinks his electric razor will show up when they have more time to look. He is at the mirror, already shaving for the evening. He flicks white lather into the sink and stretches his mouth to one side for a clear smooth run of the razor. He wants to take Ellen somewhere special to eat, he says. "What do you think?" he asks Rocky. "Seafood or French?"

Wade splashes after-shave on his face and the sweet layers of pine hit Rocky like a gut punch. "French," he tells his father, not even really knowing the word in that moment or why he says it.

As Wade and Ellen hurry to get ready, Rocky glides once through their room, and the car keys are there on the nightstand waiting for him—flashing, metallic, calling to him in the way that jewelry or a lighter calls to the solitary shoplifter. When he drops the keys quietly into his pocket, he feels nothing. He tells his father and Ellen he's going to his room to look at TV.

Instead, he goes down the elevator and out the side door of the hotel. He walks down the sidewalk and feels his skin shrinking, the keys pressing his leg each time he moves. The sun will dip behind the long, purple belt of mountains soon, though it is still unbearably hot outside. A group of older women in stretchy floral swimming suits at a nearby cocktail table wave bright Chinese fans before their faces, which send their blue-gray hair fluttering.

No real plan opens itself to Rocky. Instead, it is the dense oleanders and privets decorating the outside wall of the hotel that open to him—a large shadowy parting between branches. He bends quickly and crawls forward. Close to the ground and with the greenery shrouding him, he is surprised at how comfortable and right this place feels. The leaves turn to him and kindle tiny bursts of the last bits of sunlight. Slowly, the noise of the bushes takes over—the locusts, the lizards, the low pulsing of sap. Rocky stretches out and rubs his cheek in the cool soothing dirt. One of his hands closes over damp leaves and the other takes hold of a ball of dried roots.

Finally, in the thin mauve twilight, out on the sidewalk that stretches big as a runway from where he is hidden, Rocky spots his father's shoes—a worried pair of white canvas topsiders pacing back and forth, then halting, then moving into the grass.

Rocky reaches down and checks to see that the keys are still in his pocket, curls up, tucks a foot under the opposite thigh, then closes his eyes. He listens to his name being called again and again—a frantic singsong message that drifts away toward the pool and then farther: to rocks and weeds and moonlight and beyond—but in the darkness of a summer's night, there is no boy left to answer.

The Flannery O'Connor Award
for Short Fiction